PURPLE DEATH

And Other Stories

John Corral

ISBN-13: 9798731901796
ISBN-10: 1477123456

Cover design by: Art Painter
Library of Congress Control Number: 2018675309
Printed in the United States of America

*For Stephen King, H.P. Lovecraft, and L. Ron Hubbard,
my muses for this collection. You three entered my mind through
dreams (nightmares?) and insisted on my writing it.*

"The oldest and strongest emotion of mankind is fear, and the oldest and strongest kind of fear is fear of the unknown"

H.P. LOVECRAFT

CONTENTS

FOREWORD

This is a blend of short stories that capture thought provoking moments, daydreams and nightmares, and reality. This is what you should expect in this collection. They are an eclectic mix of stories, each unique in style, voice and story, with a wide range of genres and characters. Their sole unifying feature is that they are intended to stick in your mind. So whether you only have time to arm yourself with a very short work of flash fiction, or want to get cozy and lost in a novella, there is a story here for you

PURPLE DEATH

Death had a color all its own

Just when it seemed the world had gotten used to these periodic outbreaks of Covid, along came "Purple Death."

The latest coronavirus identified by health organizations was officially known as Covid-26 but commonly called "Purple Death" by most people because it triggered blood clotting in the temple and forehead areas of the face of those infected that turned ghostly shades of purple before they died.

Most Covid outbreaks had not been dangerous after a universal vaccine was invented that kept most people from being infected. Yet Covid-26 was different. It was highly contagious, very deadly, and the universal vaccine was not effective against it. Already it had devastated the country and killed tens of millions. How many exactly was not known. Upwards of a third of the population, perhaps a hundred million or more was the estimate. And like most of the recent Covids, it afflicted the elderly, those past sixty-five.

Little was otherwise known about Covid-26. Was it spread through person-to-person contact? Was it airborne? Did masks and other face shields help in prevention? What was known was how quickly it attacked its victims. The first symptoms were sharp pains, sudden dizziness, then darkening of the skin to the tell-tale purple color. Death came within minutes sometimes of the purple color appearing.

What was left of the country was divided by age. Those fifty or older lived perilous lives fearful of catching the virus. The mortality rate for them was more than 50%. Those younger than fifty had a mortality rate of less than 1%, and they lived relatively carefree lives undaunted by the devastation of the country due to "Purple Death."

The rock band "Purple Death" took its name from the latest coronavirus. Not particularly popular before the name change, it became the hottest band around because of its name and because all of its songs had to do with Purple Death. Its frontman and songwriter went by the moniker "P.P." —short for Purple Prince.

P.P. had been known by many other names before then since he had been around for many years and was a member of many different groups but had never hit it big until now. While happy that he was successful after so many years of obscurity, he was also arrogant. He took satisfaction in being as mean and nasty now in payback for how he was treated before becoming successful.

Because the country was effectively locked down, the group didn't travel. Instead, it played each night in its own venue, a nightclub called P.P.'s Palace. Even though they were breaking quarantine, the club drew turn-away crowds each night. It was the place to be. Still, dauntless but precautious, the club followed protocols to ensure no one who had the disease would be admitted. After all, the country was almost half depopulated now for a reason.

Those that did show at P.P.'s Palace —thousands each night— were gleeful and carefree, utterly untroubled by the fate of others not as young or as well protected from the pestilence of Covid-26. They drank, laughed, partied, and danced in an environment that was their island from the outside world. Or they secreted away into places within P.P.'s Palace, which at one time was an auto factory, and still had many areas in which to seek seclusion.

Then the government announced that a new variant of Covid-26 had been identified, one that was even more deadly and that afflicted everyone... Even the young. Lockdowns would be mandatory for 30 days.

Upon learning of this, P.P. devised a plan. He would make his club genuinely isolated from the world. He and his band, plus about up to a thousand of his most faithful fans, would take shelter within the club. The club's doors and windows would be bolted, and every means of entering or departing welded shut. With a power generator, food and drink to last for the mandatory isolation period, areas to sleep and bathe provided, the party would go on while the world outside was damned.

The club itself was redecorated in Gothic, dark, and grotesque ways... In purple, of course. The price for admission to the club? $100,000 per person, payable in gold.

The new variant of Copied-26 was as deadly as it was feared. News reports put the death counts in the millions per day. Too many to cart away or bury, the dead greatly exceeded those that still lived. Each day, each week grew the death counts. How many yet lived outside? Perhaps as few as 10 percent of the population.

What happened outside P.P.'s Palace was of no concern to those inside. They were safe, secure, and partied on. They drank, they laughed, they danced as if revelry and fun was their only purpose in life —and it was.

About the third week of the lockdown, and while the pestilence raged most furiously outside, things inside had become somewhat dull with the same activities each day. That was when P.P. decided to hold a contest. The best dancer would be chosen, and a prize given for that honor. After that, each night, another competition was held. In turn, contests were held for the best singer, the most beautiful woman, the most handsome man, and then the most grotesque. This last contest held the most interest to P.P. For he reveled in seeing the distorted, the ugly, and most disgusting in life. While the crowd had been the judges for the other contests, he would be the sole judge for that of the most grotesque.

Alas, when the contest for the most grotesque person was held, there were only two entrants. P.P. was greatly disappointed. True, they were somewhat grotesque in appearance, made more so by tattered garments and makeup that amplified less than ideal features, but were they genuinely grotesque? And there were only two.

"Is there no one else?" Asked P.P. to the crowd. "Please, someone else must come forward... Someone truly grotesque. I will increase the prize to double the amount."

The crowd grew quiet. Everyone looked around. But no one stepped forward.

"No, I will triple the prize," said P.P.

Still quiet.

"Four times!" Said P.P. "I will make it four times the prize money!"

There were hushed breaths. Surely someone else would step forward, but no one did. P.P. turned away from the crowd, much displeased.

Then, all at once, there came a buzz or murmur from the crowd, expressing that something or someone was stirring the masses. In the dim light of the club, P.P. could not tell what that was. But it appeared someone else was coming forward. The crowd was parting to let that person step forward towards him. And the crowd's expressive murmurs turned from surprise to that of fright, terror, and then of disgust.

From that crowd which prided itself on being youthful and good-looking came the very personification of grotesqueness. The figure was tall, and most eyes tilted upward to view it and then down as if in disgust. In truth, the bounds of grotesque didn't do it justice. It was far more than that. That personage touched the most profoundly unsettling emotions of all. Even those far away could see it and be repelled by it. The crowd, which had been happy moments before, was now feeling pangs of horror that they had never known before.

The figure was thin and gaunt and shrouded from head to foot in remnants of cloth like a mummy. The head was barely visible, concealed somewhat, and resembled a corpse. It was as if the figure had been buried and arose weeks after death. And on the face were the vestiges, the features of the Purple Death!

When the eyes of P.P. fell upon this image, he was seen to be confused, in the first moment with a strong shudder either of terror or dictate, but, in the next, his frown reddened with rage and anger. "Oh, my God!" He uttered. And then he collapsed.

And thus, P.P. acknowledged the presence of the Purple Death — the real Purple Death. It had come like a thief in the night. And one by one dropped those within the club. And what had been a place of revelry was now a place of death.

How the disease came to be inside P.P.'s Palace was never known. Was it carried in on some parcel of food and kept alive somehow in cold storage? Or did it sneak in hidden in the belongings or the clothing of some person? Or was it airborne and came through the air vents expected to filter all, but did not. No matter. It had entered the club. The dropping of bodies made that clear. Not all at once, but inevitably, slowly and surely. Each with the tell-tale appearance of the purple death. And the color purple —deep, lurid, and vile, was everywhere and anywhere, and did not miss anyone.

NETFLIX MAGIC

*Technology can be magical
and mysterious*

It was bitterly cold that day in March 2034 when the two young evangelists rang Peter's doorbell. They were working door-to-door in town, and a long way from their home base, Billy Bob Gram's Evangelist Ministries in Waycross, Georgia. Winters in Waycross were becoming warmer but going in the opposite direction of becoming colder in the country's northern areas.

The young evangelists would make one call on a house, spend no more than five minutes outside, and then hurry back to their motor home to get feeling again in their hands and face before they made another run at a house to spread God's word. They would always leave the engine running so that the motor home that had "Billy Bob's Ministries" painted on all sides did not freeze up.

Peter knew the routine because he had seen it before. They knocked hard on the door, rang the bell, and then looked at the camera and flashed big toothy smiles. And because most people had audio with their doorbell cameras, they said, "Morning Sir or Madam, We're from Billy Bob's Ministries. Mind if we step in and let Billy Bob Gram tell you why you need to be saved?"

The two young men waited there for five whole minutes before their watches sounded that time was up, and they ran back to their van. But not this time. Peter's voice replied, "You say you have Billy Bob with you to tell me that?"

"May we come in to explain? It will only take a minute or so," said the first young man.

"Please, may we come in?" Said the other young man.

"Again, it would only take just a moment of your time." They both looked like their parkas weren't doing them any good at all. Probably bought in Georgia for style and not locally in Fargo for this kind of cold weather.

Peter was interested. He didn't get many visitors, and because of the present cold snap, even the mail and grocery deliveries were done by drones. Just a real human face was welcome. He had been visited before by these evangelist types —whether Christian, Mormon, Jehovah's Witnesses, or whatever, going back many years. Their live presentations were usually supplemented by longer ones on a disc to put on the Netflix Magic player. It would be a VR version of Billy Bob preaching his gospel. And that would be similar to the Billy Bob Ministries Show on cable-TV that Peter never watched.

But it wasn't just being visited by actual people that interested Peter. He had another purpose in mind. His Netflix magic device wasn't working correctly, and he thought the young men might be able to help him with that. When his DVD player wasn't working some years back, two Mormons got that fixed after a short while.

When Peter released the door lock, the two young men stepped in. They expected to feel immediate warmth. It wasn't warm, just not as cold as outside. Peter stood there in a wool coat and scarf. And as if to answer the question they had on their minds, Peter said, "The furnace stopped last night. Two water pipes froze, and the toilet broke. If you need to, you know, use the bathroom, you have to use a pail. And never mind the ice on the floor there, mostly it is just from the busted pipes."

That might have been too much information for the two young men because they were rendered speechless. Peter thought a moment and then returned with his usual comment about Fargo weather, "Cold 'nuff for ya?" He reached for the bottle of Great Lakes Pumpkin Spirit Whiskey in his overcoat pocket to hand it to one of the young men. But as he took it out, he noticed it was empty. Someone had finished it, perhaps himself. He was placing it back into his pocket when it slipped and shattered on the floor. "You might think I'm drunk, but I'm not. I only wish I was. In this weather, you got to keep something in you like anti-freeze in a car."

"We don't," said Roger, one of the young men.

"Around here, even the girl scouts take a nip of something when they go door to door selling cookies," said Peter.

When there was no response from either of the young men, Peter said, "And the boy scouts have that in their 'Winter Survival' classes."

The two young men looked at each other. Was he putting them on, they were thinking.

"Cows hereabouts don't complain about farmers with cold hands if they have enough whiskey in them… In the cows, not the farmers!"

Finally, Kyle, the other young man, said, "Those are all jokes, right?"

"One more," said Peter as he clenched his teeth, trying to keep a straight face to not blow the punchline, "This ain't a historic cold. You'll know that when hell freezes over, or when the Vikings win the Super Bowl!"

Peter slapped the front of his pants when he said that and doubled over in laughter. The two young men remained rigidly upright and didn't laugh.

"You both are the most humorless guys ever," said Peter. "At least one of those jokes gets a laugh from most people.

"We are here for serious things," said Roger, followed by the Kyle who said, "To bring you the Lord's teachings, through the words of Billy Bob Gram And we should introduce ourselves. I am Kyle. And this is Roger."

"Well, I'm Peter. And if you want to get that done, you have better fix my Netflix Magic device first. It's over here."

Peter stepped into the living room from the hallway and toward the TV screen on the wall. Beneath it was a sleek low cabinet with several black pieces of equipment within it. "Here it is," said Peter, "it's the cube with the red Netflix logo on the top."

"That's not the newest model," said Roger. "Where does the disc go?"

"Speak to the Netflix Magic cube," said Peter, "it'll open for you and show you where to insert it." As he said that, a female voice said, "This is Magia. Did you have a request?"

"Yes," said Peter, "we do. I have two guests with me, and they want to know where they can insert a disc. Show them."

"You can insert a disc where the light is flashing. Do that now," said Magia.

Roger took a disc from his parka pocket, bent over, and inserted it in the back of the cube where a light glowed bright red. Immediately the cube closed, and the TV came on. Instead of a VR image projection, a series of vertical lines appeared and clicking sounds. Roger studied what appeared, shook his head, turned to Kyle, and said, "What do you make of that?"

"It's not working right."

"Yeah, but why? Have you ever seen something like that before?"

"Nope, never," said Kyle. Then, in the direction of the Netflix

Magic device, he said, "Magia, can you make it work?"

The voice said, "I am making it work."

"No, Magia, make it work!" said Roger.

The voice said, "I am making it work!"

Kyle said to Roger, "My cousin in Atlanta has one of the original Netflix Magic Cubes just like this. He says it's the best. I wonder if it isn't a problem with the TV…" And he started slipping his fingers along the edge of the TV, peering on the controls as he went, with Peter closely watching him. "When did you last replace the TV? I don't see the latest controls for VR interchangeability and interaction."

"It's been a while," said Peter. "I got this one maybe ten years ago."

"Technology has changed since then, with VR making leaps and bounds since then, and probably 90% better than it was five years ago," said Kyle.

"I'm happy to provide you with 10% of what you watched five years ago," said Magia. As she said that, a part of a female figure appeared. It was the top portion of a heavily made-up face. "Do you want to see the other 10% portions of what you watched? I have many similar movies stored."

"NO, NO!" said Peter. "We were interested in the latest discs, which apparently you can't make work."

"I can make it work. And I am making it work!" Said Magia.

"Magia, play the disc again," said Roger.

Once again, a series of vertical lines appeared and clicking sounds. Roger studied what appeared and said to Kyle, "That's maybe 10% of the vertical picture of Billy Bob cut into fine lines, isn't it?"

"Yeah, you're right. That's what it is!"

"Magia, are you out of storage? Is that why you can't show all that's on the disc?"

"I was never in storage." the voice said.

"I meant computer storage."

"I am not a computer. I am Magia."

"Magia, listen to me carefully. Is the reason why we can't see 100% of the disc image because you are without sufficient internal storage to read what is there, take those images and sounds, turn them into electronic signals, and then send them to the TV receiver that turns them back into images and sounds?

"I am Magia, and I do listen to you carefully."

"Peter, I think I know what the problem is," said Roger.

WEIRD AND HORRIFIC VISIONS

The inspiration for another's inspiration

A lonely-looking sixty-something lady boarded the Metro at the very last second. The other-worldly bluish tint of her thinning hair drew attention away from her hideous burgundy and green paisley blouse.

But only for a moment.

Glancing around, I noticed that the only open seat on the train is right next to me. Hoping that she won't notice, I adjust the newspaper in front of me.

Too late.

"Is this sssssseat taken?" Her forked tongue slithered the words as her snaggletoothed grin completed with her hideous obsidian almond eyes for attention from me.

Certain that I had seen a green tentacle lined with translucent barbs peek out from under her ankle-length skirt, I decided to play it cool. "No, ma'am," I said.

Then I rose, saying sweetly, "I'm getting off at the next stop, and you can have it all to yourself." I didn't want to get too close to her for fear that her touch would turn me into one of her kind.

After getting to the door and waiting until the train stopped at the next station, I glanced back at her. She had already interested the passenger behind her in conversation. The fool!

After exiting and looking at the Metro map, I determined that I could get to the conference faster using the Yellow Line. No reason to stay on the Blue Line where it might not be safe.

I glanced behind me to make sure I'm not being followed.

Clear.

The Yellow Line train pulled up to the platform and screeched to an impossibly quick halt. The doors opened, and a crowd of commuters rushed out. I boarded cautiously and decided that standing would allow me the greatest flexibility should a rapid egress be in order.

"Are you finished with the Sports section?" The young, upwardly looking man in the imitation Brooks Brothers suit looked up from his seat, eying the Washington Post wedged in my armpit. His eyes are stygian pools of the deepest black. Small beetle-like creatures emerge momentarily from his right suit sleeve, then burrowed back into the safe haven of cloth and flesh.

"Here, take the whole thing. I'm done." I'm wise to this guy. He'll hand it back to me, and that'll be the way for him to convert me to his kind.

At the next station, the Yuppie-looking thing leaves. That saves me having to change trains again.

A third stop without incident. I feel safe enough to venture down the aisle and take a seat.

At the next stop, three college-aged, bottle-blonde girls bounce on board. They stand near the entrance, backs turned. One of the girl's hair parts at the back of her head and a pair of ominous pincers reveal themselves. Viscous green poison drips from them.

I mutter under my breath. "Oh, for the love of Pete! My stop is next. Are they going to block my way out?"

I rise slowly, watching carefully as the pincers clatter together hungrily. As I edge toward the exit, one of the trio turns toward me and bares a mouthful of grotesquely sharp and elongated incisors.

With only nanoseconds to spare, I squeeze through the closing doors. The Conference Hotel is just across the street from the station. Streets are generally much safer, especially in the daylight.

At the Renaissance Hotel, the line for registration for the conference is obnoxiously long. Fortunately, as a keynote speaker, I don't think I have to wait in line. Being quasi-important does have its perks.

I go beyond the registration desks and look for the official in charge, Dr. Lydia Forsyth, conference chairperson. I see a tall woman and recognize her from the program guide photo. As I approach her, she seems to recognize me and strides across the room purposefully, extending her hand prematurely. I stand and wait for her to reach me.

"Oh, I'm SO glad that you made it. Everyone is looking forward to your part of the program. I don't suppose you could give me a little preview, could you?"

"What do you want to know?" I say cautiously.

"Well, you claim to have been a friend of and the inspiration behind many of H. P. Lovecraft's stories. I was wondering if you might at least give me a little hint as to that."

She does her best to appear friendly and non-threatening. She fails miserably. After all, it is rather difficult to be attracted to someone with razor-sharp talons at the end of all four limbs.

ON LEAVE WITH MY PARENTS

*The second part of my leave
was far more bizarre*

I had received a two-week pass from the Air Force and spent it with my parents over the Christmas holidays. Not together, but separately since they were divorced, one week with him and the next with her. My Dad got me first because my mom was honeymooning in Mexico with her new husband, Adolfo.

The first week hadn't ended when I got the call from my Mom on Christmas morning at about ten. "Can you pick me up?" She said. "I'm at LAX at the United terminal, and I don't think I have enough money for a taxi. And don't ask about Adolfo. I left the bastard… Good riddance!"

About two hours later, I was minutes away from the airport and called her. She didn't answer, and it went to voice mail. That happened twice more before she answered.

"Juanito, I forgot to call you. I'm sorry, but I shared a cab with someone who was coming to the Valley. I'm at my place now. So, you don't have to worry about me now. I'm fine. See you in a few days."

That was just like her. Flakey and forgetful. She hadn't changed. "Mom, I was going to spend a week with you beginning tomorrow. But since you called, I grabbed all my stuff and have it with me. I'm coming down to your place now to stay for a week."

There was hesitation on her part, then she said, "Can you make it at least two hours? He's here now, you know, the man who drove me, and we're having a drink."

"Mom, it's noon on Christmas, and you're drinking with someone you just met?"

"Make it an hour then, okay?" And before I could say anything more, she hung up.

Gloria, my Mom, has always been flighty and scatterbrain. My Dad married her when I was eight, and she was better to me than my birth mother, and that's why I always referred to her as Mom. Does she need an hour? I'll give her two, I thought. I'll stop somewhere for lunch to kill time. I settled on Denny's because nothing else was open on Christmas Day.

My Dad told me that he married Gloria, not for love but for laughter. His first wife, Lisa —my birth mother, was a religious zealot, a Catholic who went to mass every morning and took me with her until I wouldn't go anymore. She resisted the divorce because it was "against the will of God," but she had made it necessary by the way she acted.

I don't think I ever saw Lisa laugh even once. Her mother had died when she was a child, and her brother died soon after she married my father. Her brother, I was told, was gregarious and very friendly; everything she wasn't, and his death hit her hard. It seemed to snuff out what little lightness or laughter she had in her.

While they were married, my Dad spent long hours at the office working on cases and preparing for court. And when he got home, Lisa was not the escape and diversion she should have been to him. He needed frivolity, but she gave him profound darkness.

That's why he required Gloria to provide him with a real escape from his everyday existence. She was fluff and fun.

My Dad told me he had seen Gloria at a Starbucks near his office a few times, smiling and laughing with others. He decided to approach her and was so taken with her that he knew he had to marry her to be with someone so upbeat. But he didn't change his workaholic ways, and eventually, she sought out others who provided her the opportunity to be lively with them.

I got to Mom's apartment a little after two. It was a one-bedroom apartment, but it seemed much smaller than my Dad's one-bedroom because Adolfo's things were all there. It was cluttered with the accumulated possession of two lives. There were two beds, two T.V. sets, two dressers, two sets of kitchen things, and dozens of boxes with their contents spilling out onto the wood floors. He had moved in with her some months before they got married. Funny, she had lived with him all that time and still left him on their honeymoon.

I tried to find out what caused the breakup, but she wouldn't tell me. "Never ask again, she said. "Because I'm never going to tell you."

She looked slimmer than before. She was always on the thin side, but now she looked skinny, almost approaching anorexia. I didn't want to ask her about that either, even after I felt nothing but skin and bones when I hugged her after arriving. But she had a nice tan and a bright smile.

"I'm really, really glad to be home," she said after we sat on the couch. "Really, really glad." She had a habit of repeating words to emphasize a point. That hadn't changed. But repeating them three or four times was new. I hoped that wouldn't continue.

"I liked Mexico," she said. "Really, really liked it. When I retire, I might move there." I was watching her. She was looking off into space and imagining that. "Of course, I'll need to get some money together to do that, but I will, eventually."

She would say the same things about other places. On the vacations we took as a family —to Florida, New York,   Canada, and a few other places— she said the same things about them. I think it was the excitement of new places rather than whether they would be suitable for retirement.

"Would you join me there, Juanito? It doesn't take much money to live there. Not like here in L.A." She was still looking off into space and not making eye contact. In a past life, she might have been a gypsy or a pilgrim.

"Or, I might just leave now and live and work in Mexico," she said.

I sighed.

"Did you hear me?" She snapped.

"Yes. So go. You're alone now... again. So nothing is stopping you."

"—As soon as I can." She said abruptly.

"When will that be?

"In a few days... Maybe a few weeks. Who knows?"

"You would, of course."

"Don't be rude. I mean it. Really, really mean it.

"And where in Mexico would you live? In Acapulco?"

"No, not there. It's changed since I was there the last time.

Maybe in Laredo, or La Paz."

"When were you in those places?"

"Twenty years ago... maybe longer."

"So, the same as when you were in Acapulco the last time?"

"Laredo and La Paz are ancient towns and won't change. Acapulco is —or was— a made-up place... Just a sleepy fishing village until it became a resort almost overnight. Now the cartels run it."

"How's that? Did you see them?" I said

"No, we stayed at a resort. But you can feel them. I think all the resorts stay open by paying them off."

"Okay, but wherever you go in Mexico, make sure you get a roundtrip ticket," I said. "Because you don't know what it's like until you get there... As you found out on your honeymoon."

She shouts as if I have viciously attacked her. "I said not to talk about Adolfo! And I'm getting a one-way ticket wherever I go. I'm never coming back here again!"

I don't respond. And neither of us says anything for several minutes. Finally, she says, "I just had bad luck with Adolfo. Can I help it?"

I don't say anything. I don't want to mention anything about Adolfo.

"Can I help it?" She repeats with enthusiasm when I don't respond.

"Yes, you can help it. You can stay here... Where you've lived most of your life."

"Here? I'm alone now. I'm divorced from your father, and you've left now too."

"I'm just in the Air Force. That's not permanent. I'll be back."

"Back to me? You mean, to live with me?" She brightens up when she says that.

"Actually, I got along better with you than with my father," I say. "You were a good mother to me. A 'cool mom,' my friends would say. But, no, not in your apartment. At least not permanently. I could find a place close by. So neither of us would be alone."

"We used to take so many trips when you were young. Do you remember?"

"Yes, of course, I do. They were fun. And some of the best times in my life."

I am transported back to those times. Back in those years when she first entered my life. She was the mother I always wanted. She was caring, loving, and non-judgmental... the exact opposite of my real mother, who I always disliked, if not hated.

Gloria was a strikingly attractive woman back then. She was tall and classy with brown eyes that danced and a bright, perfect smile. When my father first introduced me to her, I thought I was meeting a movie star. And later, I kept a picture of her in my locker in school. I got teased about that, but I liked the attention I got when I said, "That's my Mom."

She had been married before to someone much older and quite rich. He was a "trust fund baby," a Californio, descended from one of the original land grants families from Spain that came over in the early 1800s, the Pico family. Most of their land had been sold off, with only small stretches still left in California's desert regions. But the patriarchs set up trust funds for the descendants. The trust fund that Gloria's ex drew from gave him distributions of almost a quarter-million dollars yearly. She never talked about him, except to say that the only thing he ever liked to do was count his money daily. And the divorce settlement didn't include anything tied to that trust fund.

My father had achieved much in his life on his own, which drew Gloria to him. That he also wanted to enjoy life, travel, and experience new things that she craved.

"Juanito, we should go somewhere together. Just you and I. Somewhere fun." As she said that, she began to look distractedly around the room as if she was deciding what to pack.

"You just got back hours ago," I said. "And you want to leave again so soon?" I also thought that I wanted to rest over the holidays, something I hadn't done so far. Indeed, that's wasn't possible at my father's place. Each day there was a new crisis to deal with.

At my grandfather's place, Christmas eve dinner was the low

point, a complete disaster with Melody and my father taking turns being bashed by my grandparents until Melody finally had enough. She got up, called them every swear word in Spanish she knew, then threw her plate of food on the floor and walked out. My Dad wasn't so dramatic. He flipped his plate over, bowed his head, and left. Me? I was just hungry. I took a few bites of food and shrugged my shoulders to say, What was that about? Before I left.

"Let's go to Texas!" She said. "Nowhere in particular. We'll make a grand tour of the state, from El Paso, up to Amarillo, down to Brownsville, and then to San Antonio, Austin, Fort Worth Dallas, and Houston."

"Mom, I only have a few days leave," I say. "Remember? I'm in the Air Force, and they expect me back by this time next week."

"So, don't go back. Tell them you quit."

"I can't do that. I signed up for four years and have about two years remaining."

"I'll go alone then!" She snapped.

"Are you sure? You've never been on your own."

"I have! It was that time just after my father died, and I lost my brother and my best friend from high school, all within a few months. Your father wasn't paying any attention to me, so I left for a month.

"Mom, you weren't alone... You took me with you."

That was true. After a couple of years of closeness, she and my father started drifting apart. He enjoyed his 'frivolity' with her for a time, but his work became his life again. He left her alone for long periods, sometimes weeks when he wouldn't see for more than a few minutes at the end of one of his long workdays and before he left again early the next day. All the good times and laughter with him stopped. She turned to me for company, to go out shopping, to the supermarket and department stores. I was her date for movies and entertainment. And when tragedy struck, I was who she turned to for empathy, validation, and closeness.

"I guess I forgot that part of it," she said. "Yes, you were with me; you were with me." She lay back into the couch's cushions, looked at me, and then beyond me as if remembering something. Then she said, "Vera Cruz."

That was a connection to her heritage. Her father was a Russian Jew who came to this country from Mexico with his parents and grandparents after World War II. The family had left Russia back in 1906 when the Czar was in power, weren't allowed to immigrate to the United States, and instead settled in Mexico.

I learned about that part of her background when she received her father's possessions. He had an old steamer trunk filled with things from his past. The family had lived in Vera Cruz, had a pharmacy there, and with other immigrants, opened a synagogue and religious school that became the center of Jewish life in Mexico between the two world wars. The trunk was filled with pictures of their life in Mexico and a few things from before then in Russia.

One of the things Mom liked best was a shawl that had belonged to her great-grandmother. It had been worn at her wedding and used on special occasions afterward. It was colorful and thick, with blue, green, silver, and light blue stripes, fringes, and had been woven from cotton from Israel. That same shawl was in wedding pictures of her great-grandparents. A few other images from their life in Russia were worn and tattered now and set on thick cardboard that was their distinguishing feature.

Another distinguishing feature of the Russian pictures was that no one ever smiled. In the photos from Mexico, everyone was always smiling. Maybe that's why Mom wanted to live there. Her father said parting from Mexico had been sorrowful for his parents. He remembered his mother sobbing on the day they left. She kept turning around, waving and shouting at everyone's words of love and promises that they would be back. But they never did return. In contrast, the parting from Russia wasn't so joyful.

Mom's grandparents fled Russia because he was a prominent member of the Communist Party and a fugitive wanted for political crimes against the Czarist State. He was eighteen, handsome and brilliant, and she was sixteen, non-political, and a robust woman who was taller than him by several inches. While he became fluent in English, she never did. She learned Spanish but mainly spoke in Russian. She had loved Russia and, almost in defiance, wouldn't give up speaking Russian or talking about life there in her homeland.

"Vera Cruz," she said again. "I want to go to Vera Cruz." Her voice was suddenly that of a young girl, sounding giggly, sing-song, with breathiness I hadn't heard before.

"Mom, I have only a few days," I said.

"Juanito, you would love Vera Cruz, really love it. When my grandmother was sick with cancer, she made my grandfather promise that they would return to Vera Cruz. He told her they would if she got better. But she didn't… She didn't."

There was an aching in her voice that seemed like she wanted to cross the barriers of time and space and reconnect with her heritage. I caressed her arm in comfort, and she looked at me, misty-eyed. What is she thinking, I wondered. She seldom spoke about her life before she met my Dad, except in fragments, and now it seems to be what she is most concerned with. She turns, puts her head down, and closes her eyes. Soon she is asleep. I don't wake her. I prepare something to eat from cans and read from a book I brought with me. I leave her on the couch and sleep in the bedroom.

The following day I awaken to the sounds of a news reporter on the T.V. talking about traffic. It's not loud, but I can hear him distinctly. Are the walls of the apartment that thin? I get up, use the bathroom, and then go into the living room. Mom is still on the couch where she was last night before I went to sleep. I go into the kitchen and make some coffee from instant.

"Make a cup for me," I hear her say.

When I take the coffee to her, she has a scowl on her face.

"What's wrong?" I ask.

"I can't stay here anymore. I have no life here, no one who cares... No one who cares."

"I care about you," I say.

"When I awoke, I thought I was a child again," she says. "With people around me that loved me. And then I remembered they're all gone... All gone."

"I care about you," I repeat.

She studies my face, searching for something... a loved one? A friend? Then she looks like she remembers something. She tries to speak, but nothing comes out. She clutches her chest in pain.

"Mom! What's wrong?"

"She's had another small stroke," the doctor tells me. I had her taken to the E.R., where she underwent several tests.

"Another one?"

"Yes, her MRI clearly shows that. They may have begun months ago, no telling when or what brought them on. But they have been growing in number and intensity. Her brain is riddled with them now. And they're not going to stop. I'm afraid there's nothing that can be done except to ease her pain and suffering."

"Is that the prognosis? Nothing can be done?"

"Nothing to stop them, I'm afraid. She'll continue to have them. She's still able to live on though and function, for now. But down the line..."

I cried. I don't recall ever feeling so sad as when I heard what the doctor said. I cried again when I talked to Mom.

"Don't cry, don't cry," Mom says in a caressing voice. "I'll be okay. You'll see."

I look into her eyes, which are filled with concern and tenderness. And then, after a pause, she smiles.

"Everything will be fine in Vera Cruz."

I wipe the tears away and grab her hand tightly.

"Can she travel?" I ask the doctor later. "On her own?"

The doctor shrugs. "I don't see why not. It's her choice where she wants to live out the time remaining."

"I don't believe it," Mom says, laughing when she's told about the strokes. "I lost my voice, blacked out for a minute, that's all. It wasn't much. I've had those things happening for a while now. It's just nerves. That's all."

"Mom," I say. "You've been having strokes. That's serious."

She peers into my face. "You're lying. Why would you say something like that? It's this place, Los Angeles. It's not good for me. You can't stop me from leaving it, leaving it, and going to Vera Cruz."

"If that's what you want, but be sure of it."

"I am sure —very sure, very sure."

The next day I make the plane and hotel reservations. We get ready to go to the airport.

"Where are all your things?" I ask her, suddenly noticing that all she is carrying is a small black tote bag with maybe just a couple of clothing changes.

When she went on her honeymoon, she took three large suitcases where she had packed practically everything she owned.

"I'll buy everything there... in Vera Cruz… in Vera Cruz," she says, letting the words trickle off her tongue like honey.

"Maybe this is not such a good idea," I say.

She ignores me and is delighted to be going. She promises to take her medication, kisses me goodbye for what might be the last time, and I see her go through security.

"Don't forget to call me when you arrive," I say. "And be careful with your money. I love you." My parting words.

At 4:00 p.m., I call her hotel to make sure she's gotten there okay. As I wait, I feel this mounting sense of dread.

The operator returns. "Not yet."

"Are you sure?" I ask him, beginning to panic. She should have arrived hours ago. What if she got lost? What if she had another stroke? Oh God, please have her be safe!

"Wait a minute," the operator says. "She's arrived. The information on her room was just updated."

She's breathless when Mom gets on the phone later. "I'm fine. It was the driver. He got lost." She pauses. "The weather is beautiful... Beautiful. Although Vera Cruz is very different." Her voice lowers to a whisper. "It's changed."

"In what way?"

"I'll tell you about it when I see you."

"Mom, I don't know when that will be."

"That's okay," she says. "I'm home."

HANK AND BERNIE

*At times what is not said is more
important than what is said*

Hank stepped out and closed the door behind him. Inside, the party was in its third hour, and he had to have his second cigarette. Across the pool, he could see Bernie sitting with a cigar. Hank walked towards him and said, "Want some company?

"Don't mind. Have a seat."

"Pretty nice night for May," Hank said as he took out a cigarette and lit it.

"Yeah, it is. Like Summer already."

"Made plans for vacation?"

"Julie does that. I go where she goes."

"I heard you was leaving the department. She decide that?"

Bernie didn't say anything. Instead, he drew deeply on his cigar, and it glowed red.

"You been on the force, what, twenty-five years? I thought we'd both make thirty. That was before you got remarried."

Bernie still didn't speak. They continued smoking until Jerry finally said, "Hey, I was kidding. Don't be so serious."

"I know what the guys are sayin' about Julie and me. She's the kind of gal that takes charge. Doesn't bother me. She tells me, and we do it."

"I know," Hank said.

"There's nothing wrong with that, is there?"

"Nothing at all."

"Like at the movies, some guy talks, and she tells 'em to pipe down. They pipe down."

"Yeah, 'cause she's a woman," Hank said, "if she'd been a man, she'd be hit in the mouth."

Bernie nodded his head. "She does things other people want to do. Ain't nothing wrong with that."

Hank shook his head and looked at Bernie and said, "No, nothing at all."

Bernie said, "You have to understand, Julie is all about doing the best thing. That's the way she is.

"Yeah, the best thing for her," said Hank.

Bernie looked square at Hank for the first time and said, "For both of us, otherwise I wouldn't go along with her."

Hank had been looking at Bernie but turned away and said, "So, got plans for after retirement?"

"Some… ideas really, rather than any concrete plans," Bernie said.

"What about doing private detective work? Wasn't that what you talked about doing after retirement some years back when we were partners?"

"Probably not going to happen… too risky, according to… some people."

"Really? Risky financially? Or safety-wise?"

Bernie tossed ash on the ground and said, "Both."

"And who said that?" Said Hank.

Bernie grimaced and said, "People, you know... just people." Then, abruptly, he said, "What about your vacation plans? Still going off to the Caribbean each year to score?"

TWO IRISES

The iris flower is unique

The only thing right about my wife Iris was her name. Her parents gave her that name, as many parents in her family had for generations, more out of habit more than tradition. My Iris truly deserved it. Our daughter Iris? Not so much, and she resented being given that name, and so many other things ever since, well, forever.

"We gave her that name," said my wife's parents —and I forget which one actually said that— "because the artist Vincent Van Gogh painted several famous pictures of Irises that the family purchased and then sold for enormous profits years later." That was a lie, and one of many that came from the lips of her parents as virtually everything that was said by them about Iris over the years.

Another lie told by her parents was what they said about the many Irises in their garden. And that was that Irises were renowned for their delicate nature, requiring exceptional upkeep in time and attention. In truth, of all the ornamental plants, Irises are almost self-sufficient, rarely need pruning, need little watering, and often have the staying power of weeds.

My Iris was the exact opposite. She did require great maintenance, of the kind that I was never capable of providing. Beyond the upkeep aspect, as I realized soon after we wed, I was not the one she needed to maintain her emotionally and sexually. I think sometimes that everything might have worked out so much more manageably if only she'd taken a secret lover. She did have dalliances, but never found the one that could supply what she needed emotionally, as I had. Yes, that need was mine as well, almost since our wedding. As to everything else, I provided that magnificently to her, as well as substantiating her family's wealth in investments and property accumulation far more than anyone else had. But that was in the absence of what she really wanted and needed, which, in the end, was everything in the world to her.

In the end. People use that idiom to mean when everything is considered, and not really the actual final result of something or its conclusion. But in this case, both meanings are appropriate. There is clarity now on Iris, in what she needed, in the end, and her actual end has been announcing itself for years. One might suppose I'd have figured it out and accepted the former by now more readily than the latter, but here I am, thinking it's not right, or too soon to tell, or something other than what I believe to be the truth.

Why? Because telling is the difficulty, to me and to my daughter, and the reality of what in the the end is not the result of anything I did. Still, I think I can save myself from her, my daughter, if the words come out bearing the brunt of it. Or at least I'll take what cover I can. What is it to be disdained by your one child? It is to be me.

Last year I bought her a vacation at a very nice villa in the South of France. "Are you trying to get rid of me," she asked, "even more?"

"It's not as though we live in the same state," I said.

She told me, "Exactly."

I have had to get my own psychologist to deal with my daughter's neuroses.

The other thing I do is clean my guns. I do that regularly, whether they have been fired or not, whether they need it or not. That's something that a man of action does I believe, as if I need reassurance that I am a man of action. That was something that my wife's family had neglected to have lately after many generations and the baton was passed to me in this generation. Of late my guns have been cleaned so much that I believe I can see my reflection in them as I rub them. I do that now as I wait for a call. I try not to look at the telephone, hope my daughter calls, and then that she doesn't call. I don't know which pains me the most. The timing on this is questionable, vulnerable, that is, because this is the weekend, and I am available when I wouldn't be on a weekday. At least then I would have a secretary between myself and the outside world.

Secretaries—oh!—the sentries of the office. I absolutely hate it whenever one of them leaves. Mostly to marriage, and maybe that's why it pains me. I see their names like they are carved on tombstones: Shorthand Nancy. Chirping Lisa. Winsome Sally. You were all good girls who deserved a life beyond the office routine. I'm weeping now. Again. Hell, I can't stop!

My wife is dying all the way this time.

I met my wife in a place that was a sleepy coast town most of the year, but where, for three months, the population swelled threefold, the rich mingled with the tourists that came to see them, and "the season" was the prime event. She was there that summer when I began selling properties. I was twenty-three, and I owed what success I had to my ability to instill awe in what I described. That worked because I saw awe in everything there, what I had never seen or knew existed before, and that allowed me to sell out of my league and catapult mw into the next. My product was old money New England real estate, sold to become new money New England real estate.

"Those who can't do, teach," Chauncey, two years senior to me in the company, said a few weeks in. "And those who can't teach, write. And those who can't write, write ad copy. And those who can't write ad copy, sell the product that sells itself."

"So what is it you're saying?" I asked him.

"That we're living the good life," he said, "with no clue or reason for us to do that." Then he went to go show a small mansion from which a senator was upgrading. What he said seemed probably, even if I didn't yet believe it.

But then I met Iris at a seafood place one night, met being a word I use loosely since I knew who she was already. The Adamses were a family about whom jealous people would note that husbands and wives looked like brothers and sisters. There was a lot of blondness to their hair, blueness to their eyes and blood—and eyebrows, what eyebrows, thick as hedgerows in France, and so dark they looked dyed.

She walked into the place in a silk summer dress that caught the breeze just so and outlined a ballerina figure, but without the toil and time to achieve that, and I thought about how the lushness of her eyebrows made her look like the most beautiful angry woman I'd ever seen. This quality is one eventually she'd impart to our daughter. But back then there wasn't a child, only the prospect of one.

One seat sat between Iris and me at the restaurant bar. As I pretended not to hang on her every word—the, usual, thank, you—I wished it were the type of place that set out bowls of peanuts for the patrons. We'd reach into the bowl at the same time, and she'd apologize, blush. Of course, she'd probably never gone to a place that served complimentary peanuts, and, as I'd learn, she definitely never apologized.

After two hours of clutching my wineglass, I rallied the virility to speak. "You're one drink away from being carried off on a stretcher."

"Why should I stop then, if there are stretcher bearers like you around?" Iris said. She had me from that point on. And soon I would be in her orbit and in her life.

I went to that restaurant nightly for two weeks. Each time, Iris entered with some new couture dress draped on her. I pictured her holding hundreds of dresses up before a mirror, even as she sat adjacent with her own bucket of ice chips and rosé. I didn't dare ask what she was doing drinking whole bottles herself, just watched Iris's elegant slouch and failed the tests of good taste night after night until, somehow, we connected on a level that I only dreamed could be possible.

I was a guy who didn't know chardonnay could be Burgundy, which she found to be astonishing and in need of correction, and then one day she was waiting for me in her half-empty two-seater in the restaurant parking lot. "We're going to California," she said. It wasn't a question, but I guess you could say I answered. To the airport and through the clouds spanning the North American continent we went, into cultivated vineyards of grapes, and of life; and fine linens, polished silver, and high fashion. I tried not to stare and waited for the moment she'd realize I wasn't much besides lucky.

"Who do you think I am, anyway?" I asked finally.

"Someone," she said, "who thinks I drink too much. Does it matter?" It didn't. Vicinity was enough. To be with Iris was to live the inexplicable knowingly. She knew the difference between prosciutto cotto and prosciutto crudo. Knowledge and age were never inverted in her world. Even when she is gone, I'll be grateful; she taught me everything that makes me belong now.

Our last night on the West Coast, Iris set out tiny bowls brimming with bubbles of caviar. They were brilliant tangerine and black, salty pearls enumerated on the table like a sea bath. She couldn't believe I'd never eaten caviar and had set the table merely so she could observe my face for signs of pleasure. I broke a shiny obsidian egg in my mouth and closed my eyes.

"You wonderful virgin!" she said.

I tried to tell her I wasn't a virgin, exactly, but of course she wasn't listening. She was running on into something else, then leaping off, twirling her fingers in my hair, stumbling and hugging, giggling brightly.

"Go ahead, spray me," she shrieked, handing me a bottle of champagne. "You deserve it." She was assertive with her whims, and I'd spent a lot of time that vacation apologizing for us. It occurred to me that Iris's child would inherit this wild and wonderful goddamn joie de vivre. She'd be the happiest child alive, this lengthening of a line of ecstatic possibility. It was a crazy thought, crazy to think of the wobbling future when I had everything in the world at those moments. I tried not to laugh whenever I apologized. It was impossible then to be sorry.

And now I go outside to look at her—our, soon my—Iris flower garden. My parents thought gardens you couldn't eat weren't worth much, but what did they know besides survival? They were like the people during the Depression who didn't even know as much as the people who hid money under the mattress. Iris, my plainly glamorous Iris, understood comprehensively what money could buy.

"You are the beat of my heart!" I was then. And she convinced her mother of that too. Her mother, that shift-dressed grande dame, cared so little about anyone but herself that she didn't bother to learn much about me beyond what Iris told her. Or maybe it was so that I wouldn't learn much about Iris?

That she and her husband needn't be told is a relief, though of course, when I first met Iris, it was her father who warned me about her. Whatever my daughter thinks, I didn't turn her mother into what she is, and my failures are not of the memory. More than two decades later I can still see the pink horizon as it was exactly then, Iris's hair glinting when we returned from California sunned and still a little drunk, that knotted little smile gathering her lips as she refused to take me back to my place. Her parents received fresh steaks, red and wet, bundled in good paper every Thursday. She wanted me to eat bloody meat with Adams the Sixth and the missus.

"Are you sure they want me here?" I asked in the driveway. "I wasn't even invited."

"Of course they do," she said. "You're irrelevant to their lives." I followed.

That night there were cocktails and proper mignonette on the terrace. Iris's mother, a woman whose hair seemed just that—not even kempt or unified but singular—talked about her preference for clay courts. Iris lazed on a linen chaise and smoked Silk Cut cigarettes, her father pacing with a drink in one hand and fiddling the other hand in his pocket. At one point late into the aperitivi, as her mother called the drinks, her father grabbed my arm, and a woozy envelope opened in my chest. His hands were oddly cold, and though his fingers followed slim lines, his grip was terrific. "A word, fellow?" He tightened his hand around my arm.

"Sure, sir," I said, and Mr. Adams led me to his library room, hand to my lower back in the fashion a man guides the woman he considers his own. Down the corridor, centuries of pink babies smiled painted smiles from elevated rows of gold frames. I wasn't an experienced drunk.

Unlike the rest of the place, the library let no light in at all. As soon as we crossed the threshold, my throat started seizing up with the book dust. Mr. Adams, a man who could have been thirty-five if you didn't look at the lines in his neck, flicked the hostile green glow of a banker's lamp on. He indicated a good leather chair, where I could suffocate as comfortably as possible.

"So you're after my daughter, son," he began. From his desk he pulled a flame and lit the fat brown finger of a cigar.

"Actually, she invited me," I said.

"And confident! Ha! That's the spirit." He punched the desk with the side of his hand, came around the furniture at me. I was not confident. He shook my shoulder. "And you intend to marry her?"

"It's a little early for that, don't you think, sir?" It was more and more difficult to breathe with the fumes of Cuba menacing the bibliosanctuary.

"A man of reason! By God! There are still men of reason in this age!" From his pocket, he drew a handkerchief—the man didn't deign to use tissues, for Christ's sake—wheezing and laughing. In the green glow of the lamp, his skin blossomed a brazen pinkish red. "Well, good, then. I like you, son. Wouldn't want you to get caught up with that lunacy."

"Lunacy, sir?"

"My daughter, of course."

"I don't understand," I said. You see, I didn't have a daughter then.

"Don't," he said. "The best thing that could happen is that you'd be that so-so so-and-so by next Tuesday, Mister, well, Mister what again?"

"Martin, sir."

"Martin! The man of reason!" He was nearly shouting, but also coughing, and also puffing, and also lighting.

"But sir," I said.

"'When the scourge / Inexorably, and the torturing hour / Calls us to penance!' Right, Martin?"

"Sir?"

"Martin, by God! Buck up, young buck." His hand thundered across my scapula, and he wheezed a noxious gray cloud in my face cheerfully.

"I care about Iris, Mr. Adams."

"No, no, now don't you make me worry about you again, Martin. I won't. Will not. The women: they wait! Come on now."

There was no time for questions. He led me back to the living room, where Iris and her mother, their furniture and clocks, whirled in a nauseating color wheel. I had to sit down. Her father's laugh was a hundred miles away, bending around convex funhouse mirrors. And then the twinkling shatter of a crystal snifter, the snap of WASP fingers for the help. Help was the help when it was people. I was the man of reason when the scourge inexorable and the torturing hour called us to penance. Iris took my hand in hers, and it was chilled from her drink, rubbery and thin, the alluring hand of a lunatic. What wasn't Mr. Adams telling me? Everything he knew, and more. I was a married man three months after.

I had been thinking of these things while in my back yard, among my flowering Irises while waiting for a call back from my daughter. My cell phone was in my pocket and was checked regularly for battery charge and a call —just in case I'd been amiss in either event. I had watered manually and then sat on a lawn chair beneath the kitchen window. If my daughter calls on the home phone, I'll hear it there and will get to before it goes to message mode. I called her work number, her cell and her home number. Now my work is done, and the onus is hers.

Without requiring money, she calls infrequently. Her excuse for not calling more is because she must make her own money. Growing up, I was always telling her motivational lies about how here in America you have to work hard for a good life, but all that they must have galvanized her against me for having it and not being so free with it. On that, I plead guilty. But my time away from home had more to do with her mother and not my daughter.

Here is why. I have been having an affair for the past fifteen years. It's never been about sex, though, truthfully, Iris and I rarely managed to put the ring around the rosie. Amber is a different bird than Iris, of course, but not because she is more sexually accomplished. I have tried to be fair to everyone involved, meaning I have been clear: Amber is not to love my daughter. When her credibility as a business associate was threatened by maternal greed, she was no longer allowed to see Iris; whatever Iris was, she was still our daughter's mother, and our daughter was still an Adams in lineage. This was when Iris was a child. The problem *au courant* is that a few months ago I decided Iris was adult enough to be told. Evidently, children are never old enough to understand their parents' affairs.

"Your business associate?" she asked.

"Actually no, but yes," I said. It had been wise to call, rather than commit the awkwardness in person. In the bright light of my own breakfast nook, I could pull on my hair without the gesture being interpreted in the quiet malice of my daughter's criticism.

"False identity," she said quietly. "Is that what you mean?"

"Correct."

"Men are the curse of the womb. No wonder Mom . . ." she said, the rest of the sentence dissolving in tears before she hung up. When I tried her again, she didn't answer, and she still doesn't know that chronology verifies my relative innocence. What I've heard from her since is a single letter.

The telephone rings now, and for a minute I close my eyes. I reach out to pluck a flower. She loves me. She loves me not. She loves me. She loves me not. Angry, yes, but she loves me probably, or I am her father at least. I get up to answer the phone.

Inside, I brush my hand over the crinkles of a silk lampshade and look out the window. When she was furnishing the house, Iris made me close my eyes and lifted bouquets of flowers to my face. I told her what the smells pictured for me. The best pictures were how we chose our garden. Her stomach was growing then. She'd stopped drinking, seemed somehow younger, and I was less afraid of her. When her parents said they'd never seen her so healthy, I knew they meant because of me. I can't explain the spell after the baby was born. Iris had always been a woman who was hard to know. After the birth, impossible. She cried in the empty tub all day. She was convinced the baby was staring at the mole on her cheek. We'd gotten the wrong baby, she said. One day Nancy, the help, called me at work and told me I'd better get to the hospital. Iris had thrown herself out the fourth story. Money hasn't bought her out of the vegetative state. It's a slow countdown to death. *Trois, deux, un.* I pick up the phone and keep looking outside. Hydrangea: a trail of snow angels.

"Brian?"

Jesus.

"I thought you were Iris."

"It's Amber," explicably, "so I take it she doesn't know about her mother yet?"

"I've been maintaining the flower beds," I say.

Amber clucks her tongue. "That sounds like a euphemism." According to the doctors, Iris is awake but they cannot establish her awareness. The distinction is lost on me. When it comes to the diagnosis, I consider myself an agnostic, meaning Amber has not been allowed to sleep over, just in case. I've kept the VHS tapes and shoulder pads, so that the day Iris woke, these years could feel like a nap. She'd return with a trace of the decade she'd left intact.

"I have responsibilities, Amber."

"You only say my name when you're angry," she says.

Amber, I think. Amber!

"Now I want you to take a big, calming breath and count to ten, focusing on positive energy flowing through your relaxed muscles. I know you, Brian, so I know you're holding a lot of tension in your shoulders right now—even without seeing you!"

"My wife is dying, Amber. I think I deserve to be angry."

"You don't need to rub it in," she says.

"Rub what in?"

"Your wife," she says.

After Amber hangs up, I begin boxing Iris's toiletries to take to the garbage bin in the garage. Iris is the most kempt woman in Intensive Care by far. Before she threw herself out the window, she always wore red nail polish and rubbed essential oil on her elbows. With the understanding that some patients spontaneously emerge from the vegetative state, I continued the regimen, which was how I met Amber—then Amber the Avon Lady—and one day after I'd been buying her product for several months, she appeared at the office to show me the new skin care line.

I was surprised at the location on which she wished to demonstrate the creamy texture of the moisturizer's revolutionary pore-refining properties. What I will say is this: the advertisements do not lie; there was something revolutionary that day. I'd call it relief. But it wasn't so revolutionary that I gave up on Iris, whom I have preserved as *primus inter pares*, off the books and on.

After the toiletries, there are the garments. In her bedroom, I lay out Iris's silk nightgowns over the bed. I cannot fit her size, but I draw one onto each of my arms. The sense of coolness regardless of temperature is the magic of the textile. There is the false liquidity of course too, the aqueous, shimmering weave that seems poured. You are Iris, I tell myself, looking in the mirror, but I realize, sweating suddenly, that the joy of opulence is now lost on me.

In my estimation my daughter Iris has never learned to enjoy pleasure the way my wife Iris did, which is why when she was younger, she was a miserable little girl and now is a miserable woman. But you cannot make a diesel car drive on *Dom Pérignon*, and what I give is never enough. I have never tried to buy love, but I have always been generous with my daughter. It's not about commerce *per se*. For example, two weeks ago I sent a really beautiful Stradivarius for her birthday even though she doesn't even play violin yet. The point was: you're a year older, but it's not too late.

So how do you tell your daughter her mother can't be hoped for anymore? She will have my head.

I don't blame Iris for her mother's turn toward defenestration, but still I waited four days, that is, until this morning, to read Iris's letter. There was recovery time to consider; a bad bout with Iris can leave me in the hole for days. So when I woke up I made myself a quick toasted sandwich, sat down in the good armchair in the living room, and got brave with the paper knife.

"Dad," the letter began. "I got your gift, which would be thoughtful if I played violin. It was a gesture. Sometimes I think the reason I became an artist was to make objects into a mother for myself instead of the other way around, which is my life, though I know this is tritely Freudian. My childhood belongs to Ollie, and I am left asking who will be my father for the rest of my life. Sometimes I believe you only care about your own comfort and salesgirls, but then I remember all these years with Mom, and I wish I knew you. Sincerely, I."

It's true that I'd left her with my nephew Ollie often when she was a child, but how could she claim him as her father? I wondered if my best recourse wasn't to ask him to talk to her. If he were my proxy, maybe she'd listen. Though I'd rarely seen him over the past ten years, he'd always had a way with Iris. And yet the mention of Freud made me uneasy as her father—not that I thought she wanted to know me in the Shakespearean sense—but because you don't bring Freud into the conversation unless your misery reaches intelligent pathology, the most frightening pathology of all. I didn't know what to respond.

I never did get to determine my position though, because then Eleanora, one of the home nurses, knocked on the door to tell me she had noticed Iris was breathing funny. "Funny like bad," she told me. "Bad-oxygen-levels funny, Mr. Brian," she elaborated.

"I've never heard of that kind of funny," I said. "You ought to get yourself a thesaurus. And what is it you do if not keep my wife from breathing unfunny?" There was a suggestion of pity across

Eleanora's face, but after we got Iris to the hospital she didn't sit with me in the waiting room. That suited me fine. Lisa or Nancy would never have allowed this to happen.

It's odd looking at pictures of expensive watches in the unflattering light of a hospital, but when money has failed you in the most important way it can, that is, health, it is nice to know there is still something it can do for someone. So I paged through a magazine as I waited for a diagnosis. A Mercedes, slick suits, and a few thousand words on the New Black later, the doctor emerged. I noticed he had a small crucifix tattooed on his neck, and the entire time he spoke, I kept staring at it, pretending it was a good omen.

"I'm sorry," he said. "But at this stage there's nothing we can do."

"What stage?" I asked.

"You should attend to arrangements, Mr. Martin."

"That wasn't what I asked."

"It's amazing she's survived this long," he said. "And you should be proud that it's been largely due to the diligence of your care. But at her age, in her condition? There's only so much that can be done now."

"There has to be more than only so much to be done," I said. "You aren't even sorry. You ought to wish you went to Harvard. I'm sure they know what to do in these situations at Harvard."

"I did go to Harvard," the doctor said. "And I am sorry."

When I look in the mirror, I see a man holding his wife's night-gowns and sniffing her cold cream. He knows he has to be fair, and he knows fair is telling his daughter things he wouldn't believe himself. Another man would drink a drink or buy a new car, but the world of things seems to diminish in substance when I think that maintaining the luxuries of my wife's youth for her eventual reawakening has been for nothing. I can look back at my entire life, the investments and property flips, the hardball tactics, and it's a number of lucrative mistakes. Somewhere in there is Iris, the last Adams, she of Freudian hatred. Blessed be the disdain of a daughter. I dial and close my eyes.

"Hello? Dad?" she says, two rings in.

"Yes, this is he," I say. "Speaking." I rub my thumb over a dark-blue negligee.

"Did you get my letter?"

"I did, I. That's how you signed it, I remember: I. And just because you're given a name doesn't mean you have to keep it. A violin either." I've always been impoverished of nonchalance, and the notes of false casual sound ridiculous as soon as I speak. Iris was the breezy one. Iris, I tried, Iris. "But I called because your mother, well. What I mean to say is something, a development, has occurred."

"So she's dead?" Jesus. Maybe this is some kind of generational gap, this unadorned honesty. For a moment, my throat starts sticking to itself. I need a glass of water.

"Well," I say.

"Dead or not, Dad? Come on."

"Not!" The silk, I realize, has gone warm in my hands. I wring it one way and the other.

"Then what's the development?"

My head is departing from my body. I'm looking down at my life from above and go woozy like I'm staring down off the roof of a skyscraper. Taking a sip of water, I choke and hack it back up.

"Sick or wrong life?" Iris asks.

"Wrong life."

"'Wrong pipe,' I said," she says.

It's difficult to start, but once I do I'm unstoppable. I explain about the appalling diction of Eleanora "Funny" Funes, the doctor and his baffling suggestion to arrange—"as though death were a bouquet!" I evoke the unapologetic defeatism of the diagnosis, prognosis. I tell her I don't trust a man with tattoos on his neck. In finale, I allude to my doubts about the current quality of education provided at Harvard University. And when there's nothing else to say, I start crying. For a moment, we just listen to each other breathe. We listen to each other being alive. My aliveness is louder than hers, with the shuddering tears, but hers is like Iris's in its mysterious softness.

"Dad," she says finally. "It's going to be okay. Nothing can be worse than the last twenty-three years."

"Twenty-three years is your entire life," I say.

"I know," she says slowly. "Which is why you need to stop hoping and start living."

"Living!" I say. "You're talking like a crazy person. What do you mean, 'living'?"

She clears her throat. "I mean let her go. Marry that woman. Take vacations. Be happy."

"Your mother makes me happy."

"My mother hasn't made anything in two decades. And the last time she did, look how well that turned out." She's talking about herself.

"If your mother could hear you right now."

"But she can't, Dad. She never has. And neither have you."

"She is the beat of my heart!" I say.

"Then who is Amber? You have to be fair to her."

"Fair?" I say. "What is fair about any of this?"

"Nothing," she says. "But I want you to be happy."

"And since when have you allied with the other woman?" I ask.

"Since I realized she's not the other woman," Iris says. "She's the woman who you've been in a relationship with for the past twenty years. You can't just use people for sex. We aren't just bodies. Only Mom is just a body."

"It has not been twenty years."

"Yeah, and she's your business associate, Dad." But wasn't she? It had always been an even exchange of minor special survival imperatives. I want the world: my wife and our daughter, that rarefied pearl of life.

"After your mother," I say, "I could love no one ever again."

"One day," my daughter says, "I'll be no one." And when she hangs up the phone, I know this is in so many ways how it ends.

AN OCCURRENCE NEAR OCOTILLO JUNCTION

In the last seconds of life… an abbreviated history flashes before your eyes.

I took my eyes off the road for just a few seconds. The FM station was playing a song from the Eighties, and I wanted to check the title and artist, which would appear if I punched the audio function and looked at the station display. It was just the briefest of moments, I'm sure. But in that time, the semi on the other side of the road turned toward me and came into my lane; although it may have been me that did that, I'm not sure.

Jerking the wheel, I probably overreacted. I was moving too quickly for the approaching corner, and there wasn't much of a shoulder. I already felt the kick of the tires in the gravel along the edge of the road as I avoided the collision. Stomping the brake pedal to the floor, I heard the rubber squealing against the pavement as I made a desperate attempt to turn the corner. Even before the spin started in the few feet of light brown dirt that cushioned the turn, I had lost control.

Another split second, and I might have made the turn, and maybe my car wouldn't have slipped into the guardrail, only halfway through its rotation. The metal crunched with the sudden impact, and my forehead bounced off the side window. Screeching metal bent and supports popped in protest of the suddenly added strain of stopping my car from falling to the valley below.

In the last seconds of your life, an abbreviated history is supposed to flash before your eyes. For me, it started in that first second of darkness after my head recoiled from the window, like a slide show with half-moving, half-frozen memories.

Chasing my father's disappearing footsteps in the soft sand at the ocean's edge or standing beside him and holding his hand as a wave receded and sucked the sand out from under my feet. In the final slide, I looked up at his face, features too dark in shadow, with the sun like a hero halo behind his wind-blown hair.

As the sun streamed back in through the windshield and my opening eyes, I felt the depth of his loss for the first time.

Metal buckled beneath me, and I felt my car shift further on its tilt. It was only on two of its wheels, but I found an explanation exceedingly difficult for my mind to grasp. Out through the driver's side window, a rocky projection seemed poised to catch my car when it fell onto its side. I thought that it should just continue the fall so that I could reorient myself and exit the crippled vehicle. Already my mind seemed to be clearing, and as my car finished rolling over the guardrail, it was at the last moment that I understood there was a drop to that projection.

Whether it was the void of unconsciousness or in the seconds of the fall, I couldn't say.

Walking along a dirt road as the sun was setting in front of me with the taste of an old-fashioned fireball searing my tongue... Sweat drops forming in the red clay at my feet as I crouched, fist in the leather of my baseball glove, watching the pitcher's arm hurl the ball towards the plate... Pushing off the wooden dock with a fishing rod in my hand as my grandfather leaned into the oars to pull the boat out onto the stillness of the lake, the stale smell of the life jacket at once unbearable and irreplaceable... The sweet smell of summer, as the tractor rolled across the lawn and freshly cut grass blended with the salt air of the marsh.

Jolted by my car landing on its roof, I was pulled against the confines of the seatbelt that kept me from leaving my seat. A bounce and the C.D.s from their holder were among the loose objects inside the car floating past me, spinning and sliding without a sense of up or down. Snapped in another direction by a collision with a more solid object, I felt the crumbling of the roof and sides. Glass shattered as a branch stabbed through the windshield, tearing into the fabric of the passenger's seat. Then another plunge, replacing the violence with the subtle sensation of weightlessness, of falling.

Running stride for stride, bumping shoulder pads with the shorter wide receiver until I was in front of him and the pass fell into my hands, as though thrown to me... Stopping short and turning to run the interception back, picking out the blocks I needed, seeing the field so perfectly clearly... The awkward lurching of the car and patient cursing of my father, as I tried to figure out how to work the clutch while rolling on a hill in our neighborhood... The sensual exploration of a tongue in an open-mouthed kiss, my fingers tangled gently in her hair as she looked up at me... My buddy and I walking the old abandoned railroad tracks for the last time, our fingers hooked through the plastic rings of six-packs, contemplating the water running under the bridge out to the sea.

A tree arrested the fall, battered metal wrapping around the trunk from the force of the collision. But the tree refused to give up its tenuous hold in the Arizona desert, and I sat with my eyes closed in my seat, feeling the blood trickling down my nose to the corner of my mouth. A bitter metallic taste that, sweetly, meant I was still alive. My lungs strained to open for a breath, and my left arm hung limply below my elbow, hand numbed by the disconnected bones floating in the muscles of my forearm. Sitting absolutely still, I waited for the moments necessary for my mind to catch up with the body that had fallen off the cliff. Fog clouded the edges of my vision, tunneled only on what was straight in front of me.

Unhooking the seat belt, I crawled carefully across the center console and away from where my car bent around the tree. The passenger door fell open as I pushed with my good arm. Stepping out onto the solid ground, I found it felt as though it was moving. My vision pulsed in and out of focus, images rotating slowly to the right. I took a couple of staggering steps forward and collapsed, unable to register the fall quickly enough to put my hands up. I was pushing myself up again, managing another step before the ground tilted up at me.

Gathered on the front steps of the house, drinking beer and watching girls walk by... Tailgating in the parking lot long past kickoff, knowing our defense would give up the lead anyway... Ski trips to the mountain with sleeping bags covering the available floor space in the cabin and empty beer cans lining the countertops... Dragging the others out onto the slopes for lessons in the art of flying in powder, hangover, or not... Camping trips out in the desert, sleeping on blankets in the open air around the dying embers of the fire.

I was shaking my head, feeling as though the scene in front of me was playing on a scratched DVD that skipped forward quickly and then back again. Sitting on the ground, I was looking back at the wrecked car, unable quite to understand when I had hit that tree. Or where the road had gone. Indeed, it didn't look like there was a road anywhere within my sight. I looked up at the blue sky above, where a few pieces of metal twisted out from the hill and shone in the fading sunlight. The small pieces of glinting metal looked like the tinsel that would hang from a Christmas tree.

Cooking steaks on the grill after a day of skiing Taos, I look up as she opens the gate to the yard, brushing a strand of hair behind her ear. She hands me another Sam Adams on the porch of Charlie's Place, fingertips touching lightly... A first date on the mountain, leaning against me as we rode the Kachina lift, ponytail swinging with the rhythm of bashing bumps on Al's Run... Soft, strawberry-scented hair catching on the whiskers along my jaw as she looks up for our first kiss. In my memory, her features are distorted.

The sun has set behind the mountain as I begin to understand where I am. My leg is bleeding from above the knee, and much of the skin below has been colored dark red, making it impossible to guess how far the cut ran. Blood seeping into the tissues around my injuries produces a collective throbbing that seems steadier than the heartbeat pumping it. Pain is as consistent as the drone of conversation in a crowded room until the mind attempts to eliminate it as background noise. Breathing is difficult. Hobbling to my car has already confirmed that the cell phone doesn't have a signal down here. One shoe is missing, and even through the sock, I can see the ankle's swelling. Somehow the other injuries have drowned out the sensation of the sprain.

A tarantula walks out into view from behind a cactus with soft sand-colored legs, and I wonder where the truck driver has gone. Why didn't he stop to see what happened to the car?

Kayaking off the Gulf side of Key West and she is following me into the saltwater streams that connect through the center of the island... Looking over the side at the tropical fish that swim by... Taking pictures with a waterproof camera, of the heron sitting alone in the corner of the salt pond, of me paddling out under the bridge, of her in her bikini laughing at the sky... The sharpness of the coral fragments on bare feet along the shore at the state beach, swimming out to the breakers... Sitting with her in my arms and watching the sun go down over the ocean, the cruise ship setting sail across our view and down to the Mexican coast... The night breeze is coming in through the window, watching her sleep, curled on my chest.

I can't bring her features into focus. The harder I try to stare at her, the blurrier they become. In the darkness in the desert, the stars are truly uncountable. In my current state, the stars are shivering when I try to look up at them. Occasionally, the sides of the valley will light as a car traveling one way or another will point its headlights out into the desert. I hold my breath as they slow to make the corner, hoping one will notice something about the skid marks on the road, the bent and twisted guardrail, anything. They continue to drive on by.

Strolling through Boston on the Fourth of July, along cobblestone streets... Grabbing a bucket of crab claws at the Barking Crab, introducing her to the pleasure of a lobster roll... Spending a reflective moment at the tomb of Paul Revere, having a pint in J.J. Foley's, we spent the day walking hand in hand... Heading to the Esplanade, to watch the Pops and the fireworks. In the darkness, I am unable to make out her face.

As I sit on the valley's hard rock floor, she is setting up the apartment in L.A., our first place together. I had chosen to drive out with the last pieces of my life from my parents' house in Boston, as she drove some of her stuff out from New Mexico. Just a momentary lapse of concentration has me at the bottom of this valley, instead of in a hotel tonight, instead of sleeping in the arms of my wife tomorrow, in our first home.

The memories come faster, almost blurring. Some are just quick snapshots; some are fragments of home movies where the film has aged with the passage of time, half-moving, half-frozen moments. Still, a few are slower. These are clearer.

Sitting on a blanket in the grass, we watch the rockets race into the night sky over the Charles... Exploding in colors of sparks, some the patriotic red, white and blue.

The lights of another car slow and stop.

A flashing red and blue pattern lights up the sky... I'm holding her back against my chest, watching the fireworks over her head... From the corner of my eye, I see the reflection in the black Glass of the Hancock tower... I whisper dirty things I want to do to her into her ear.

A flashlight shines down from above.

She turns her head to share the moment with me, as the fireworks ex-

plode, reflected in the river's water, and the two of us watch the sparkling cascade like a wave up the side of the building... Another moment, one of many that I can recall, somewhere in the forest near the Appalachian Trail, walking among Autumn leaves... Still another portion of the trail, this time in winter, with snow flurries... A festive moment, standing in a crowd, watching what everyone else was watching but with our own unique perspective.

From the solitude around me, a tree branch brushes my face. Or is it a tree branch? Maybe it is her hand on my cheekbone.

A voice softly whispers with the breeze. "I'm here, baby," she says. "It's okay."

"I know, babe. I know," I say out loud. A voice calls down from the edge of the cliff.

I can see her now as she crouches before me. Her eyes are a dark green, skin tanned with a spattering of freckles across her nose from the time outside in the desert sun, hair a light sandy blonde... Eyebrows turned upward, wrinkling her forehead in concern... Gentle lips brush against mine.

"I'm sorry, babe," I say.

"It's okay," she replies softly.

I can still see the stars even though my eyes have closed. She eases to the ground beside me; her shoulder rests lightly on my own. Her head tilts up at the night sky, and I can feel her hair drift across my face in the breeze.

Standing with our heads tilted together, foreheads touching gently, lips brushing, as I run my hand across her cheek, she smiles. "It will only be a week apart," she says.

The searchlight pointed down into the valley blurs the images in my mind, and I expect to be blinded by its glare. Instead, I can see the stars, in the emptiness of the night, as I close my eyes for the last time.

JIM'S FRENCH
HORN FATHER

From two different worlds,
two different fathers

Jim Richardson was a sensitive boy who grew up a farmer's son until "the accident." After that, everything changed. On a Spring day under a big upstate New York sky, his father Bill Richardson ran over and killed his brother, Jules. Even at the last moment, his father could have prevented Jules's death by slamming on the tractor brakes. But, his father was slow-witted, as everyone said, was unable to think, or, more correct, thought unclearly. Jim watched it happen, as he would, again and again, watch it happen in his mind, with nearly undiminished intensity and clarity, all his life.

Jim and Jules were riding where they should not have, as both of them knew, and their father knew as well, on the cultipacker, a two-ton implement lumbering behind the tractor, crushing new-plowed ground. Jim was twelve, his brother, Jules, was ten. The scream came not from Jules, who never got a sound out, but from their five-year-old sister, who was riding on the fender of the tractor, looking back. When Jim turned to look, the huge iron wheels had reached his brother's pelvis. His father kept driving, reacting as he would to a half-crushed farm animal and imagining, in the same stab of thought, that perhaps his son would survive. He did not.

Jim was nearly destroyed by it. He had been a talkative boy growing up, constantly chattering about something, but after that day, he said little and kept to himself. He had shared a bedroom with his brother but said he couldn't continue to sleep there. His father insisted that he would. After that first night, his mother found him lying on the floor, crying, unable to stand up. "You can sleep in the barn," his father said.

The father, Bill Richardson, was as insensitive as his son Jim was sensitive and unintelligent as his son was intelligent. They also differed significantly in aspirations. Jim was by nature a dreamer. It showed in the books he favored, his drawings, and his diary entries. His father cared for only his work as a farmer and very little else. Jim loved his sister and brother and his parents. And would not consciously have been able to hate his father even when Jim knew, as indeed he did, his father had murdered his brother.

Jim could not help blaming his father, though consciously he blamed only his father's unintelligence and—so far as his belief held firm—God. Jim's mind swung violently at this time, reversing itself almost hour by hour, from desperate faith to the most savage, black-hearted atheism. Every sickly calf, every sow that ate her litter, was a new, sure proof that the religion he'd been taught to follow was a lie. Yet man's brain and body were too perfect and could only be engineered by a creator and not the result of random chance, according to Darwin. He was unable to decide, one moment full of rage at God's injustice, the next moment wracked by doubt of his existence.

Though he was not ordinarily a man who smoked, his father would sometimes take out one cigarette and smoke it leisurely after his evening meal. That also changed. He would sit up all night now, or move restlessly, hurriedly, from room to room, chain-smoking Lucky Strikes. Or he would stare blankly at the moon for hours on end, a cigarette in his mouth trying to see something there, or to forget something, both morbidly the same in his eyes, and meant to put behind him how Jules had once been his favorite to take over the family farm. Bill Richardson would also think about suicide so that he wouldn't have to decide anything more about the future.

Previously, the only decisions Bill would have to make were where he would go hunting or fishing next. He hated decisions, feared them, and mixed fear and anger for the reason not to decide the big questions beyond the next time to fly off to hunt or go fly-fishing with friends. On the moonlit nights when he thought of his future, he discovered, invariably, no reasons how the damage his suicide would do to his wife and the children remaining.

Sometimes Bill would forget all for a while by abandoning his role as husband, father, and farmer, and all responsibilities for decisions, by engaging in love affairs. At this time, Jim Richardson's father was still young, still handsome, and well-known for his physical prowess growing up a gifted athlete in school. He won races to loud applause, ran savagely over defenders in football, and thrashed wrestlers into early submission. He was a star athlete in everything he undertook —as long as it didn't take much beyond physical strength and stamina. He had opportunities to pursue other girls but chose to go steady with someone who tutored him in order to be able to get grades sufficient to let him play sports. Out of school, his wife was no longer needed for that.

Bill was now so full of pain and doubt that women's hearts flew to him unbidden. He became, with all his soul and without cynical intent, a hunter of women, trading off his sorrow for the sorrows of wearied, unfulfilled country wives. He would often be gone from the farm for days, abandoning the work to Jim and whoever was available to help—some neighbor or older cousin or one of Jim's uncles. No one complained, at least not openly. A stranger might have condemned him, but no one in the family did, certainly not Jim, not even Jim's mother, though her sorrow was increased. Before the accident, Bill Richardson had always been a faithful man, one of the most fair-minded, genial farmers in the country. No one asked that, changed as he was, he do more, for the moment, than survive.

As for Jim's mother, though she'd been, before the accident, a cheerful woman—one who laughed often and loved telling stories, sometimes sang parodies of T.V. commercials or ads on the radio to make her husband and children laugh—she cried now, nights, and did only as much as she had the strength to do—so sapped by grief that she could barely move her arms. She comforted Jim and his sister, Susie—herself as well—by embracing them vehemently whenever new waves of guilt swept in, by constant reassurance and extravagant praise, frequent mention of how proud some relative would be—once, for instance, over a drawing of his sister's, "Oh, Susie, if only your great-aunt Lucy could see this!"

Great-aunt Lucy had been famous, among the family and friends, for her paintings of families of lions. And Jim's mother forced on his sister and himself comforts more permanent: piano and, for Jim, French-horn lessons, school and church activities, above all an endless, exhausting ritual of chores. Because she had, at thirty-four, considerable strength of character—except that, these days, she was always eating. And because, also, she was a woman of strong religious faith, a woman who, in her years of church work and teaching at the high school, had made scores of close, for the most part equally religious, friends, with whom she regularly corresponded, her letters, then theirs, half filling the mailbox at the foot of the hill and cluttering every table, desk, and niche in the large old house—friends who now frequently visited or phoned—she was able to move step by step past disaster and in the end keep her family from wreck. She said very little to her children about her troubles. In fact, except for the crying behind her closed door, she kept her feelings strictly secret.

But for all his mother and her friends could do for him—for all his father's older brothers could do, or, when he was there, his father himself—the damage to young Jim Richardson took a long while healing. Working the farm, plowing, cultivating, disking, dragging, he had plenty of time to think—plenty of time for the accident to replay, with the solidity of real-time repeated, in his mind, his whole body flinching from the image as it came, his voice leaping up independent of him, as if a shout could perhaps drive the memory back into its cave.

Maneuvering the tractor over sloping, rocky fields, dust whorling out like smoke behind him or, when he turned into the wind, falling like soot until his skin was black and his hair as thick and stiff as old clothes in an attic—the circles of foothills every day turning greener, the late-spring wind flowing endless and sweet with the smell of coming rain—he had all the time in the world to cry and swear bitterly at himself, standing up to drive, as his father often did, Jim's sore hands clamped tight to the steering wheel, his shoes unsteady on the bucking axle beam—for stones lay everywhere, yellowed in the sunlight, a field of misshapen skulls. He'd never loved his brother, he raged out loud, never loved anyone as well as he should have. He was incapable of love, he told himself, striking the steering wheel. He was inherently bad, a spiritual defective. He was evil.

So he raged and grew increasingly ashamed of his raging, reminded by the lengthening shadows across the field of the theatricality in all he did, his most terrible sorrow mere sorrow on a stage, the very thunderclaps above—dark blue, rushing sky, birds crazily wheeling—mere opera set, proper lighting for his rant. At once he would hush himself, lower his rear end to the tractor seat, lock every muscle to the stillness of a statue, and drive on, solitary, blinded by tears; yet even now it was theater, not life—mere ghastly posturing, as in that story of his father's, how Lord Byron once tried to get Shelley's skull to make a drinking cup. Tears no longer came, though the storm went on building. Jim rode on, along with the indifferent, murderous machinery in the widening ten-acre field.

When the storm at last hit, he'd been driven up the lane like a dog in flight, lashed by gusty rain, chased across the tracks to the tractor shed and from there to the kitchen, full of food smells from his mother's work and Susie's, sometimes the work of two or three friends who'd stopped by to look in on the family. Jim kept aloof, repelled by their bright, melodious chatter and absent-minded humming, indignant at their pretense that all was well. "My, how you've grown!" the old friend or fellow teacher from high school would say, and to his mother, "My, what big hands he has, Betty!" He would glare at his little sister, Susie, his sole ally, already half traitor—she would bite her lips, squinting, concentrating harder on the mixing bowl and beaters; she was forever making cakes—and he would retreat as soon as possible to the evening chores.

He had always told himself stories to pass the time when driving the tractor, endlessly looping back and forth, around and around, fitting the land for spring planting. He told them to himself aloud, taking all parts in the dialogue, gesturing, making faces, discarding dignity, here where no one could see or overhear him, half a mile from the nearest house. Once all his stories had been of sexual conquest or of heroic battle with escaped convicts from the Attica Prison or kidnappers who, unbeknownst to anyone, had built a small shack where they kept their captives, female and beautiful, in the lush, swampy woods beside the field. Now, after the accident, his subject matter changed. His fantasies came to be all of self-sacrifice, tragic stories in which he redeemed his life by throwing it away to save others more worthwhile. To friends and officials of his fantasy, especially to heroines—a girl named Margaret, at school, or his cousin Linda—he would confess his worthlessness at painful length, detailing all his faults, granting himself no quarter. For a time, this helped, but the lie was too blatant, the manipulation of shame to buy love, and in the end, despair bled all color from his fantasies. The foulness of his nature became more apparent and more evident in his mind until, like his father, he began to toy—dully but in morbid earnest now—with the idea of suicide. His chest would fill with anguish as if he were dreaming some nightmare wide awake or bleeding internally. His arms and legs would grow shaky with weakness until he had to stop and get down from the tractor and sit for a few minutes, his eyes fixed on some comforting object, for instance, a dark, smooth stone.

Even from his father and his father's brothers, who sometimes helped with the chores, he kept aloof. His father and uncles were not talkative men. They never told jokes, though they liked hearing them, and because they had lived there all their lives and knew every soul in the county by name, nothing much surprised them or, if it did, roused them to mention it. Their wives might gossip, filling the big kitchen with their pealing laughter or righteous indignation, but the men, for the most part, merely smiled or compressed their lips and shook their heads. At the G.L.F. feedstore, occasionally, eating ice cream while they waited for their grist, they would speak of the weather or politics; but in the barn, except for "Jimmie, shift that milker, will you?" or "You can carry this up to the milk house now," they said nothing. They were all tall, square men with deeply cleft chins and creases on their foreheads and muscular jowls; all Presbyterians, sometimes deacons, sometimes elders; and they were all gentle-hearted, decent men who looked lost in thought, especially Jim's father, though on occasion they'd abruptly frown or mutter, or speak a few words to a cow, or a cat, or a swallow. It was natural that Jim, working with such men, should keep to himself, throwing down ensilage from the pitch-dark, sweet-ripe crater of the silo or hay bales from the mow, dumping oats in front of the cows' noses, or—taking the long-handled, blunt wooden scraper from the whitewashed wall —pushing manure into the gutters.

He felt more community with the cows than with his uncles or his father when he was there. Stretched out flat between the two rows of stanchions, waiting for the cows to be finished with their silage so he could drive them out to pasture, he would listen to their chewing in the dark, close barn, a sound as soothing, as infinitely restful, as waves along a shore, and would feel their surprisingly warm, scented breath, their bovine quiet, and for a while would find that his anxiety had left him. With the cows, the barn cats, the half-sleeping dog, he could forget and feel at home, feel that life was pleasant. He felt the same when walking up the long, fenced lane at the first light of sunrise—his shoes and pants legs sopping wet with dew, his ears full of birdcalls—going to bring in the herd from the upper pasture.

Sometimes on the way, he would step off the deep, crooked cow path to pick cherries or red raspberries, brighter than jewels in the morning light. They were sweeter then than at any other time, and as he approached, clouds of sparrows would explode into flight from the branches, whirring off to safety. The whole countryside was sweet, early in the morning—newly cultivated corn to his left; to his right, alfalfa and, beyond that, wheat. He felt at one with it all. It was what life ought to be, what he'd once believed it was.

But he could not make such feelings last. No, he thought bitterly on one such morning, throwing stones at the dull, indifferent cows, driving them down the lane. However he might hate himself and all his race, a cow was no better, or a field of wheat. Time and again, he'd been driven half crazy, angry enough to kill, by the stupidity of cows when they'd pushed through a fence and—for all his shouting, for all the indignant barking of the dog—they could no longer locate the gap they themselves had made. And no better to be grain, smashed flat by the first rainy wind.

So, fists clenched, he raged inside his mind, grinding his teeth to drive out thought, at war with the universe. He remembered his father, erect, eyes flashing, speaking Mark Antony's angry condemnation from the stage at the Grange about politics, the Republicans this and that. His father had seemed to him, that night, a creature set apart. His extended arm, pointing, was the terrible warning of a god. And now, from nowhere, the black memory of his brother's death rushed over him again, mindless and inevitable as wind or wave, the colossal cultipacker lifting—only an inch or so—as it climbed over the shoulders, then sank on the cheek, flattening the skull—and he heard, more real than the morning, his sister's scream.

One day in August, a year and a half after the accident, they were combining oats—Jim and two neighbors and two of his cousins—when Susie came out, as she did every day, to bring lunch to those who worked in the field. Their father had been gone, this time, for nearly three weeks, and since he'd left at the height of the harvest season, no one was sure he would return, though as usual, they kept silent about it. Jim sat alone in the shade of an elm, apart from the others. It was a habit they'd come to accept as they accepted, so far as he knew, his father's ways. Susie brought the basket from the shade where the others had settled to the shade here on Jim's side, farther from the bright, stubbled field.

"It's chicken," she said and smiled, kneeling.

The basket was nearly as large as she was—Susie was seven—but she seemed to see nothing unreasonable in her having to lug it up the hill from the house. Her face was flushed, and drops of sweat stood out along her hairline, but her smile was not only uncomplaining but positively cheerful. The trip to the field was an escape from housework, he understood; even so, her happiness offended him.

"Chicken," he said and looked down glumly at his stiff, tanned arms black with oat-dust. Susie smiled on, her mind far away, as it seemed to him, and like a child playing house, she took a dishtowel from the basket, spread it on the grass, then set out wax-paper packages of chicken, rolls, celery, and salt, and finally a small plastic Thermos, army green.

She looked up at him now. "I brought you a Thermos all for your-self because you always sit alone."

He softened a little without meaning to. "Thanks," he said, touched, noticing that she bowed her head in the way a much older girl might do, troubled by thought, though her not quite clean, dimpled hands were a child's. He saw that there was something she wanted to say and, to forestall it, brushed flying ants from the top of the Thermos, unscrewed the cap, and poured himself iced tea. When he drank, the tea was so cold it brought a momentary pain to his forehead and made him aware once more of the grating chaff under his collar, blackening all his exposed skin, gritty around his eyes—aware, too, of the breezeless, insect-filled heat beyond the shade of the elm. Behind him, just at the rim of his hearing, one of the neighbors laughed at some remark from the younger of his cousins. Jim drained the cup, brooding on his aching muscles. Even in the shade, his body felt baked dry.

"Jim," his sister said, "did you want to say grace?"

"Not really," he said and glanced at her.

He saw that she was looking at his face in alarm, her mouth slightly opened, eyes wide, growing more expansive, and though he didn't know why, his heart gave a jump. "I already said it," he mumbled. "Just not out loud."

"Oh," she said, then smiled.

When everyone had finished eating, she put the empty papers, the jug, and the smaller Thermos in the basket, grinned at them all and said good-bye—whatever had bothered her was forgotten as soon as that—and, leaning far over, balancing the lightened but still-awkward basket, started across the stubble for the house. As he cranked the tractor, she turned around to look back at them and wave. He nodded and, as if embarrassed, touched his straw hat.

◆ ◆ ◆

Not till he was doing the chores that night did he grasp what her look of alarm had meant. If he wouldn't say grace, then perhaps there was no heaven. Their father would never get well, and Jules was dead. He squatted, drained of all strength again, staring at the hoof of the cow he'd been stripping, preparing her for the milker, and thought of his absent father. He saw the motorcycle roaring down a twisting mountain road, the clatter of the engine ringing like harsh music against shale. If what he felt was hatred, it was terrible, desperate envy, too; his father all alone, uncompromised, violent, cut off as if by centuries from the warmth, chatter, and smells of the kitchen, the dimness of stained glass where he, Jim, sat every Sunday between his mother and sister, looking toward the pulpit where in the old days his father had sometimes read the lesson, soft-voiced but aloof from the timid-eyed flock, Christ's sheep.

Something blocked the light coming in through the cowbarn window from the west, and he turned his head, glancing up.

"You all right there, Jimmie?" his uncle Walt said, bent forward, nearsightedly peering across the gutter.

He nodded and quickly wiped his wrist across his cheeks. He moved his hands once more to the cow's warm teats.

A few nights later, when he went in from chores, the door between the kitchen and living room was closed, and the house was unnaturally quiet. He stood a moment listening, still holding the milk pail, absently fitting the heel of one boot into the bootjim and tugging until the boot slipped off. He pried off the other, then walked to the icebox in his stocking feet, opened the door, carried the pitcher to the table, and filled it from the pail. When he'd slid the pitcher into the icebox again and closed the door, he went without a sound, though not meaning to be stealthy, toward the living room. Now, beyond the closed door, he heard voices, his sister and mother, then one of his aunts. He pushed the door open and looked in, about to speak.

Though the room was dim, no light but the small one among the pictures on the piano, he saw his father at once, kneeling by the davenport with his face on his mother's lap. Susie was on the davenport beside their mother, hugging her and him, Susie's cheeks stained, like her mother's, with tears. Around them, as if reverently drawn back, Uncle Walt, Aunt Ruth, and their two children sat watching, leaning forward with shining eyes. His father's head, bald down the center, glowed, and he had his glasses off.

"Jimmie," his aunt called sharply, "come in. It's all over. Your dad's come home."

He would have fled, but his knees had no strength in them, and his chest was wild, churning as if with terror. He clung to the doorknob, grotesquely smiling—so he saw himself. His father raised his head. "Jimmie," he said and was unable to say more, all at once sobbing like a baby.

"Hi, Dad," he brought out and somehow managed to go to him and get down on his knees beside him and put his arm around his back. He felt dizzy now, nauseous, and he was crying like his father. "I hate you," he whispered too softly for any of them to hear.

His father stayed. He worked long days, in control once more, though occasionally he smoked, pacing in his room nights, or rode off on his motorcycle for an hour or two, and seldom smiled. Nevertheless, in a month, he was again disappearing at night, and sometimes for longer... for a day, then two or three days. His father's eyes no longer flashed; he no longer had the look of a god. Even his gestures were submissive, as pliant as the grass.

Though tears ran down Jim Richardson's face—no one would deny that his father was still effective, still the leader of the family, still a farmer, still a father, he was no longer Jim's father. Jim ignored what his father said, his opinions, and scorned the way his father spoke when he told them as if each were some new woman, his father some mere suffering sheep among sheep, and scorned the way Susie and his mother looked on smiling, furtively weeping, heads lifted. Jim's heart would swell with rage, yet he kept silent, more private than before. At night he'd go out to the cavernous haymow or up into the orchard and practice his French horn. One of these days, he told himself, they'd wake up and find him gone.

He used the horn more and more now to escape their herding warmth. Those around him were conscious enough of what was happening—his parents and Susie, his uncles, aunts, and cousins, his mother's many friends. But there was nothing they could do. "That horn's his whole world," his mother often said, smiling but clasping her hands together. Soon he was playing third horn with the Seneca Falls Civic Orchestra, though he refused to play in church or when company came. He began to ride the Bluebus to Rochester, Saturdays to take lessons from Avi Primakova, "the General," at the Eastman School of Music.

Primakova was seventy. He'd played principal horn in the orchestra of Czar Nikolai and at the time of the Revolution had escaped, with his wife, in a dramatic way. At the time of the purge of Kerenskyites, the Bolsheviks had loaded Primakova and his wife, along with hundreds more, onto railroad flatcars, reportedly to carry them to Siberia. In a desolate place, machine guns opened fire on the people on the flatcars, then soldiers pushed the bodies into a ravine, and the train moved on. The soldiers were not careful to see that everyone was dead. Perhaps they did not relish their work; in any case, they must have believed that a wounded survivor would have no chance against wolves and cold weather in a place so remote. The General and his wife were among the few who lived, he virtually unmarked, she horribly crippled. Local peasants nursed the few survivors back to health, and in time the Primakovas escaped to Europe. There Primakova played horn with all the great orchestras and received such praise—so he claimed, spreading out his clippings—as no other master of French horn had received in all history. He would beam as he said it, his Tartar eyes flashing, and his smile was like a thrown-down gauntlet.

He was a barrel-shaped, solidly muscular man, hard as a boulder for all his age. His hair and mustache were as black as coal except for touches of silver, especially where it grew, with majestic indifference to ordinary taste, from his cavernous nostrils and large, dusty-looking ears. The sides of his mustache were carefully curled, in the fashion once favored by Russian dandies, and he was one of the last men in Rochester, New York, to wear spats. He wore formal black suits, a huge black overcoat, and a black fedora. His wife, who came with him and sat on the long maple bench outside his door, never reading or knitting or doing anything at all except that sometimes she would speak unintelligibly to a student—Primakova's wife, withered and twisted, watched him as if worshipful, hanging on his words.

She looked at least twice the old man's age. Her hair was snow-white, and she wore lumpy black shoes and long black shapeless dresses. The two of them would come, every Saturday morning, down the long marble hallway of the second floor of Kilburn Hall, the General erect and imperious, like some sharp-eyed old Slavonic king, moving slowly, waiting for the old woman who crept beside him, gray claws on his coat sleeve, and seeing Jim Richardson seated on the bench, his books and French horn in its tattered black case on the floor beside him, the General would extend his left arm and boom, "Goot morning!"

Jim, rising, would say, "Morning, sir."

"You have met my wife?" the old man would say then, bowing and taking the cigar from his mouth. He asked it each Saturday.

"Yes, sir. How do you do?"

The old man was too deaf to play in orchestras anymore. "What's the difference?" he said. "Every symphony in America, they got Primakovas. I have teach them all. Who teach you this? The General!" He would smile, chin lifted, triumphant, and salute the ceiling.

He would sit in the chair beside Jim's and sing, with violent gestures and a tremendous upward leap of the belly to knock out the high B's and C's—Tee! Tee!—as Jim read through Kopprasch, Gallay, and Kling, and when it was time to give Jim's lip a rest, the General would speak earnestly, with the same energy he put into his singing, of the United States and his beloved Russia that he would nevermore see.

The world was at that time filled with Russophobes. Primakova, whenever he read a paper, would be so enraged he could barely contain himself. "In all my age," he often said, furiously gesturing with his black cigar, "if the Russians would come to this country of America, I would take up a rifle and shot at them—boof! But the newspapers telling you lies, all lies! You think them dumb fools, these Russians? You think they are big, fat pushovers?" He spoke of mile-long parades of weaponry, spoke of Russian cunning, spoke with great scorn, a sudden booming laugh, of Napoleon.

Jim agreed with a nod to whatever the General said. Nevertheless, the old man roared on, taking great pleasure in his rage, it seemed, sometimes talking like a rabid communist, sometimes like a fascist, sometimes like a citizen helplessly caught between mindless, grinding forces, vast, idiot herds. The truth was, he hated both Russians and Americans about equally, cared only for music, his students, and, possibly, his wife. In his pockets, in scorn of the opinions of fools, he carried condoms, dirty pictures, and grimy, wadded-up dollar bills.

◆ ◆ ◆

One day a new horn he'd ordered from Germany, and Alexander, arrived at his office—a horn he'd gotten for a graduate student.

The old man unwrapped and assembled it, the graduate student looking on—a shy young man, blond, in a limp gray sweater—and the glint in the General's eye was like madness or at any rate lust, perhaps gluttony.

When the horn was ready, he went to the desk where he kept his clippings, tools for cleaning and repairing French horns, cigars, photographs, and medals from the Czar and pulled open a wide, shallow drawer. It contained perhaps a hundred mouthpieces, of all sizes and materials, from raw brass to lucite, silver, and gold, from the shallowest possible cup to the deepest.

He selected one, fitted it into the horn, pressed the rim of the bell into the right side of his large belly—the horn seemed now as much a part of him as his arm or leg—clicked the shining keys to get the feel of them, then played. In that large, cork-lined room, it was as if, suddenly, a creature from some other universe had appeared, some realm where feelings become birds and dark sky, and spirit is more solid than stone.

The sound was not so much loud as large, too large for a hundred French horns, it seemed. He began to play now not single notes but, to Jim's astonishment, chords—two notes at a time, then three. He began to play runs. As if charged with life independent of the man, the horn sound fluttered and flew crazily, like an enormous trapped hawk hunting frantically for escape. It flew to the bottom of the lower register, the foundation concert F, and crashed below it, and on down and down, as if the horn in Primakova's hands had no bottom, then suddenly changed its mind and flew upward in a split-second run to the horn's top E, dropped back to the middle and then ran once more, more fiercely at the E. This time burst through it and fluttered, manic, in the trumpet range, then lightly dropped back into its home range and, abruptly, stopped in the middle of a note. The room still rang, shimmered like a vision.

"Good horn," said Primakova and held the horn toward the graduate student, who sat, hands clamped on his knees, as if in a daze.

Jim Richardson stared at the instrument suspended in space and at his teacher's hairy hands. Before stopping to think, he said, "You think I'll ever play like that?"

Primakova laughed loudly, his black eyes widening, and it seemed that he grew larger, heavenly and demonic at once, like the music; overwhelming. "Play like me?" he exclaimed.

Jim blinked, startled by the bluntness of the thing, the terrible lack of malice, and the truth of it. His face tingled, and his legs went weak as if the life were rushing out of them. He longed to be away from there, far away, safe. Perhaps Primakova sensed it. He turned gruff, sending away the graduate student, then finishing up the lesson. He said nothing, today, of the stupidity of humanity. When the lesson was over, he saw Jim to the door and bid him good-bye with a brief half-smile that was perhaps not for Jim at all but for the creature on the bench. "Next Saturday?" he said as if there might be some doubt.

Jim nodded, blushing.

He began to breathe more easily at the door opening on the street, though he was weeping. He set down the horn case to brush away his tears. The sidewalk was crowded—dazed-looking Saturday-morning shoppers herding along irritably, meekly, through painfully bright light. Again he brushed tears away. He'd been late for his bus. Then the crowd opened for him, and with the horn cradled under his right arm, his music under his left, he plunged in, starting home.

A DANGEROUS LIFE

No one makes it out alive

The long shadows crept across the valley floor until they reached me in my perch. Good. I would be relieved soon. I flexed my back and stretched my muscles. It was another shift when nothing happened. No one is sneaking in, no one trying to escape. Nothing. Not even something I killed and could take back and eat. Danny and I have been doing this every Wednesday, our time at the barrier since… Well, so long that I can't remember when we started. Has it been a year already?

Danny has it worse than me. He's draped in camouflage and lies on his belly the entire shift. If they come up the dry gulch, which is possible, Danny would be a sitting duck if they spotted him and started shooting. I'm triple that distance and sit up high on a ledge with a carbine, supposedly backing him up, which is total bullshit, and we both know it. He put me in a safe position. I can see the road and cover that but can't see the gorge—no use pointing that out or arguing with him. Dan's hard as iron. Ex-military special forces and ex-cop, he's happiest when things are stacked against him. This assignment is voluntary, and we risk our lives for $50 an hour that the Association is reluctantly paying to do something about the outsiders on this stretch of road.

They want the "good guys" to get through, primarily commercial trucks that carry the supplies we need to stay alive, but also those who left just before things shut down and want to get back to where it's reasonably safe. It might not be that safe here, but it's a hell of a lot better than it is in the cities. There are also those we can't let out, something the Association worries about because they might tell the world about us, and we can't let that happen.

The roads are the worse since life as we used to know it started breaking down. A busload of people got held up at gunpoint on the interstate last month. They had an escort, but it didn't do them no good. They nailed the cop first before stopping the bus. Nobody else was killed, but everything they had was stolen. No more buses our way since.

I yawned. I was up early this morning when I answered the phone at six or so. It was Myrna who called to tell me that Andre was back in town. I made some coffee, drank a cup, dunked a roll in it for breakfast, then strapped on my piece and headed for her place mad as hell. I drove that stupid fucking junkie out of town yesterday, gave him money for a room and something to eat, and told him to stay put until I got in touch with the consulate to ship him home. No matter, he came back.

Andre is seventeen years old and stoned every day, on the run from a father who beats him but still wants him back. He's persona non grata in this place for breaking into cars and talking shit about the Great One and the Association. He long ago got the idea that I was someone who hated them as he did and could trust me. I tried to persuade him otherwise or that he wasn't my responsibility because I let him stay at my place once. But like a stray dog, he keeps coming back.

Tammy was waiting for me at Myra's. Bizarre chick, maybe 30 years old, but acts like a teenager. I met her last year at one of the pothead parties above the Iguana Restaurant, smoking pot with some wealthy newcomer from Michigan, a guy we ultimately had to throw out for being such an asshole. Tammy was probably sleeping with him to get high, which is what she only cared about, and he had an endless supply of the good stuff. I couldn't blame her if she were.

He had a massive bag of big green buds. I smoked a lot of pot last year, as everybody else did. It was just before things shut down and one of those golden summers to remember. The place was a haven for the worst of the best, so to speak —the dot com million-aires who got too rich too soon, stockbrokers who made money while losing other people's money, and airhead supermodels from New York who were the prizes in life to all the others, and what went on with drinking and doing drugs till dawn.

Tammy was a mystery I never bothered to unravel. She spoke with a whistle, like an old guy with false teeth. Not bad looking, voluptuous, thick brown hair that she kept behind her ears and spilled over soft muscular shoulders. A little plush around the middle. Not my type, but she kept popping up wherever I went, always asking if I knew anyone who could give her a job. She wanted to stay. So I took her to Rick, and she handled the counter in relief when he stepped out. She also sold trinkets on the street for a while. Then she found work at Olga's doing night shift duty, filling in for relief and washing dishes.

Tammy lived in one of the squatter places —if you call that living, a dirty abandoned motel called The Easy Rest. No running water and no working toilet. I didn't usually associate with people from there, but Tammy didn't care about that or too much else. She was better alone, she said, and nobody bothered her there. She was pretty odd that way, and she stayed more or less permanently there. Illegal of course, according to the Association. There were plenty of places approved by the Association for outsiders, ex-pats who came in on three-month visas extended by the Associ-ation and never went home. When the Association Police made sweeps, they'd find such people and throw them out eventually, but not so much anymore. Even our closed society is breaking down now.

That's why assholes like Andre are still around. Tammy had him stay with her for a while, and she even had to throw him out. This day when he saw me, he lifted an eyebrow and pointed to the sky as if he was going to fly away real soon. He was slumped over a table in the sun with a half dozen empty brown bottles, two of which were horizontal in a puddle of buzzing flies.

I flicked the safety off my weapon and strode over to his table. Andre must have heard me crunching gravel and looked up. "Tex..." he mumbled stupidly, "I couldn't stay there, so I came back."

I ordered him to get up, and when he opened his mouth to spew another paragraph of bullshit excuses, I rapped him on the shoulder and the top of his head for good measure. We marched over to my car, and I shoved him in the back seat. He had enough sense to keep his mouth shut while we drove to the Association's jail, behind their meeting place. "Lock him up and keep him here until the transport comes," I growled at the guy on duty and threw a $20 bill on the desk. He agreed; no questions or paperwork needed.

Soon he'll be on his way out, on the daily transport and then a plane to his mother in Moscow. She was worried when I last talked to her, maybe a month ago now; he belonged there and in school. With a bit of luck, things'll turn out right for him. Once in a while, these sad-sack soap operas turn out halfway right. Thinking about that, I forget more important things, like not getting my head shot off.

Bang - THWAP - a chunk of bark hit my head! Another loud bang and my upper arm stung, and I jump for the ground; a disorganized, flailing leap made more difficult with a rifle in my hands that ended in a hard bellyflop that smashed the wind out of me. That was all I remember.

I woke up with Danny ripping my shirt apart." Where are you hurt?" he asked angrily. I said I was hurt everywhere. He picked me up in a fireman's carry and started running. "Put me down!" I tried to shout. He was bouncing my guts, making everything hurt a hell of a lot worse. So I smacked him in the kidneys, to no effect. He kept running.

We got to the hillside, where he flopped me down on the ground, out of breath and gleaming with sweat like a racehorse. "Can you ride?" He panted. I nodded, and he pulled me up and sat me on my Harley. I fumbled with my key, and he helped me with that too. Then he put my rifle back in its case, jumped on his ride, and said," Follow me!" He gunned his machine and headed straight up a rough jungle path over the hills to the beach. I began to get the idea we were in trouble and had to be elsewhere pronto.

We raced across wet sand with the tide coming in. In an hour, our tracks would be gone. At Rock Point, Danny stopped, ran, and threw his Sig-Sauer and Steve's .45 in water that was too dangerous to surf or swim. He waved me in the direction of town, like a stern traffic cop at the scene of a car wreck, then spun around and went the other way. That was the last I saw of him. A week later, they called me to pick up his cycle. It was found in the river near Tres Gauchos, about twenty miles away, out of gas.

I watched Danny disappear into the jungle and melted slowly into a pile of sore bones and trembling flesh across the steering bar of a red hot machine that was starting to sputter. It took a long time to find the reserve tank knob. I burned my hand on the engine with a wrong guess.

I decided I needed a drink and pulled into the little slot at the front of The Dice Bar in town. It took a long time to stand up and throw my bad leg over the saddle, then switch the motor off. I could barely walk, just limped through the wide front arch. It was Happy Hour, fifteen or sixteen lazy drinkers and loud music. I stumbled against a table and made it to the bar's open end near the back wall. Tony grabbed the Dewars and poured a drink for me. I asked for more ice and fished a couple of cubes out of the glass with my left hand, and pressed them against the rip in my sleeve near the shoulder.

"You okay, Tex? You look like shit," he said. Unless my eyes were playing tricks on me in the dim light, the bar owner was sweating and shaking. Tony was the one who looked like shit tonight.

"Never mind me. What's up with you?"

His hands twisted a bar rag as he leaned over to talk in a whisper like it was unsafe. "Jesus, Tex, I have to have a gun. Can you get me one? I know what the rules are, but there were three guys in here a little while ago. Never saw 'em before. They were casing the joint, and I have to stay open till late tonight. It's a game night."

I nodded and unbuckled the fanny pack around my waist, laid it on the bar, fumbled with the zipper, got my cuffs out, and put them in a back pocket. "It's a single action," I explained. "You have to cock it every time. Loaded with .22 magnum. Do yourself a favor and get some .22 shorts. It kicks like hell unless you hold the barrel down with your other hand. Can you remember that?"

Tony nodded. "Yeah. Thank you. How much?"

"Nothing. If anyone asks, I was never here."

I drove through town in second gear somewhat inaccurately and made it home, got off, and started to fumble with the gate latch. My wife came running across the patio in that cute way girls have of tiptoeing at top speed. I got back on the Harley, and she opened the gate, then latched it shut behind me when I was in.

"What happened?" she wanted to know. I let her help me inside, into a bedroom, and then onto the bed, where she took off my clothes. There was a little cry of anguish when she saw the deep red groove on my upper arm. I vetoed the doctor idea. "Just treat it like a burn," I mumbled and then blacked out, safe and snug behind a perimeter wall and cameras, with a partner who was better and faster with a long .38 than I was.

I think I slept a night and a day and another night before I hobbled around a little and sat on the couch a while to eat soup and a sandwich. The next day I felt good enough to go downtown for a newspaper. The crowd at the grocery store froze and gave me a wide berth at the checkout. The store owner asked politely if there was anything 'Mr. Tex' needed. I gave him a buck for the English language paper and opened it.

It was there, page one: four dead, all of them known to be Association-related. A beer truck driver saw what happened near Quebrada Bridge from a distance and called it in. But he got into trouble because the cops found a pistol in his cab that "may have been recently fired and reloaded." He was booked for resisting arrest.

And there was another part of the story. A rental car was found near a ditch next to the bridge. It belonged to Tammy Oberlin, and friends said that she was on her way to see a baby doctor in the capital. She was two months pregnant. It was unknown if the group that stopped her knew that before they shot out her tires, raped and beat her, leaving her for dead. But she wasn't dead — not then anyway. Broken vertebrae bounced in an ambulance for three hours before she got to a hospital, where she died from infection after surgery.

It still makes me sick whenever I think about it. But, it's a dangerous life these days, and no one makes it out alive.

RECOGNITION AND ROSEN

Bernie Rosen stared at the dollar figure on the contract that had just been delivered by messenger. It confirmed what his agent said to him an hour before. He would be paid two million two hundred thousand dollars for his screenplay. Even less the ten percent commission, that left him with over two million dollars for his script. On top of his last script, for which he got a cool million, this was confirmation that he was not a flash in the pan.

Walking to the Starbucks on the corner from his condo, he felt lighter than air, almost as if his feet didn't touch the ground. All that money for only a month's work. He almost smiled at this slight resentment he felt at paying his agent the two hundred thousand. Of course, his agent negotiated that sum so that Bernie would still be left with two million dollars. A slim, good-looking woman smiled back at him as she held the door for him to enter Starbucks.

Did she know him? Or knew of him? He did not turn, fearing she would stop and begin the conversation that by now was unbearable for him. "I only wanted to tell you that it's the best movie

I've seen, well, ever." In that part of West Hollywood, he was well known and had become somewhat of a celebrity over the past five years since he moved there from the Valley. Everyone in the area seemed to be in some way associated with the movies, either in front of the camera or behind it.

He kept his head down as he walked toward the line of people waiting to order while resolving once again to develop some gracious set of replies to those people who might recognize him, who, after all—at least some of them—were sincere. Whatever he said must be special; after all, he was a writer. And not only a writer, but the most successful writer in Hollywood working today. But he knew he would always stand there tongue-tied like a jerk. He could craft words but not say them himself. Yet, for some reason, he wouldn't mind being recognized today, at a loss for saying something interesting or not. He was too happy, too ashamedly content, and satisfied with himself.

On the counter display case were cookies, muffins, and scones. He paused. Would he buy one to have with his coffee? It's been years since he had to question whether he had enough money to spend on a two or three-dollar muffin. My God, he thought, I could buy them all! I could buy all the muffins in all the Starbucks in the states! Maybe even the world! Barriers of price were suddenly worthless.

In the glass of the display case, he saw his weary eyes, his round, sad face and narrow beard, his sloping shoulders and wrinkled shirt; for the King of Hollywood writers, he thought, you still look like a failure. He was next in line to order, and a hand grasped his forearm with annoying proprietary strength and turned him to an immense chest, a yachtsman's sunburned face with a chic, narrow-brimmed hat on top.

"You wouldn't be Bernie Rosen?"

"No. I look like him, though."

The man blushed under his tan, looked offended, and nodded.

"Well, you could be his brother, anyway."

Bernie sat in a far corner of the Starbucks, where he usually sat and wondered if he needed to have a muffin and coffee so close to dinnertime. He looked at his watch. It was a quarter to six, and the dinner meeting was for seven-thirty. He tried to remember if there was a book store in the neighborhood. Maybe he could spend time there instead. Or perhaps he could take in a movie. But there wouldn't be time for a whole film unless he happened to come in at the end. Still, he could afford to pay for half a movie. Sure, he would do that.

He walked out of the Starbucks and headed toward the promenade. A couple stared at him as he passed. His eye fell on displays of properties for sale in the front glass of a real estate office. The properties were all in the million-dollar-plus category, unavailable to him before, but not now. He could afford any of them now. He smiled... Any of them.

He wondered why he had been reluctant to move out of his furnished apartment even though he could have afforded to buy his own condo years ago. Would he have to dress better? Eat out at better places? Be with people more educated, more successful? He thought of shaving his beard. But then, he thought, they won't recognize me. He smiled. I am hooked. So be hooked, he muttered, and, straightening up, he resolved to admit to the next interloper that he was, in fact, Bernie Rosen and happy to meet his public.

On a rising tide of honesty, he remembered the years in the Valley, the shabby apartments, smallish and ill-furnished, his notes spread on desktop as he constructed script after script, and the mirror in his bathroom where he would look at his morose eyes, wondering when and if they would ever seem as unique as his secret fate kept promising they would someday be.

◆ ◆ ◆

On the promenade, so vibrant and alive with people, he headed toward the movie theaters; his hands clasped behind his back. Two blocks west, he got to them, two movie theaters on opposite sides. It was nearing dusk, and the lights had been turned on. The first theater had four screens with nothing beginning soon. Across was the theater with six screens. Nothing there as well that began before seven. Were any of his movies playing? No. But it was nice having to look to find that out.

When his first script sold and was turned into a movie, he became intimately familiar with the process, involving himself with everything associated with producing the film. His input was welcomed since the producers and director were new as well. He was there when the movie was cast and gave green lights to everyone hired. He was also involved with hiring others, from the costume designer to most of the technicians. He was part of the team. Not so with his last movie. On that, he was intentionally shutout, and he knew it. But by then, he didn't want to go through all of it again. Most of it was going after the money. And the more needed, the greater the strategies, persistence, and enthusiasm — and less honesty. Finding, meeting, and closing prospective investors on the movie's merits was the most challenging part of the process.

The worse part of the last script sold was that he was even cut out of the changes. Not those that happened on set, but before production began. No script was ever final, and getting it to the point of an actual working script meant making changes. It was on those that he was no longer involved with. "Script doctors" hired by the producers were. Though the lawyers had extracted "locked script" provisions on his script's sale, they were ignored. "Your time is better spent writing other scripts," he was told. Still, being present when the actors spoke his lines, and the director, cinematographer, set designers, and technicians; in all, maybe thirty-five people, had been joined together by his story, their lives changed and in a sense commanded by his words, was wonderfully fulfilling.

Being told, "Your time is better spent writing other scripts," only begged the question. And in his heart, in a hollowed-out place, stood a question mark: Was it possible to write another script? Thankfully he thought of his wealth again, subtracted ten per-cent commission from the movie purchase price, and divided the remainder over the next thirty years. He wouldn't starve ever again, he thought. Then he angrily swept all the dollars out of his head. An older man stopped a few feet from him and said, "Hey, Rosen!" Several others nearby noticed. So he lifted his left hand a few inches in a crimped wave—like a Royal, and gave a half-hearted motion towards them all. An unexplainable disgust pressed him toward a facial sign of recognition as well. Then he turned and walked on towards the restaurant meeting place. He would be early but not have to endure more of the same.

He had a vague recollection of eating in the Palatine restaurant years ago. He had been trying unsuccessfully to sell a TV pilot script. "Rosen, if you would only follow a plotline...." Before he got there, he noticed a Chinese restaurant. It would probably be empty at this hour, and it wasn't elegant. He pushed open the bright-red lacquered door and thankfully saw that the bar was empty and sat on a stool. Two girls were alone in the restaurant part, talking over teacups. The bartender took his order with-out any sign of recognizing him. He settled both arms on the bar, purposefully relaxing. The Scotch and soda arrived. He drank, examining his face, which was segmented by the bottles in front of the mirror. Cleanly and like a soft blow on his shoulder, the realization struck him that it was getting harder and harder to re-member talking to anyone as he used to in years past and all his life before his scripts had sold, before he had come on view.

Even now, in this empty restaurant, he was already expecting a stranger's voice behind him, and half wanting it. Crummy. A longing rose up in him to face someone with his mind on something else; someone who would not show that charged, distorted pressure in the eyes which, he knew, meant that the person was seeing his printed face superimposed over his real one. Again he watched himself in the mirror behind the bar: Rosen the morose, Bernie bleak and peevish. Sullen, but a millionaire with movies being seen on five continents. Setting his drink down, he noticed the soiled frayed cuffs on his once-tan corduroy jacket and the shirt cuff sticking out with the button off. A distant feeling of alarm; he realized that he was meeting his director and producer and their wives at the restaurant and that these clothes, to which he had never given any thought, would set him off as a character who went around like a bum when he had two scripts sold for record amounts.

Thank God anyway that he had never married! To come home to the old wife with this printed new face—not good. But now, how would he ever know whether a woman was looking at him or at "Bernie Rosen" in full color on the Variety cover? Strange—in his dreams of success, he had envisaged roomfuls of girls pouring over him when his movie scripts sold, and now it was almost inconceivable to make a real connection with any women he knew. He summoned up their faces, and in each, he saw calculation, that look of achievement. It was exhausting him, the whole thing. Months had gone by since he had so much as made a note. What he needed was an apartment in Brentwood or West Hollywood somewhere, among people who were in the business and moderately successful. But would they know him as successful? He sipped his second drink. His stomach was empty, and the alcohol went straight to the back of his eyes, and he felt himself lifted up and hanging restfully by the neck over the bar.

The bartender, a thin man with a narrow mustache and only faint signs of Chinese features, stood before him. "I beggin' you pardon. Excuse me?"

Bernie raised his eyes, and before the bartender could speak, he said, "I'm Bernie Rosen."

"Ha!" The bartender pointed into his face with a long fingernail. "I know. I recognizin' you! On ET show, right?"

"Right."

The bartender now looked over Rosen's head toward someone behind him and, pointing at Rosen, nodded wildly. Then, for some reason whispering into Rosen's ear, he said, "The boss invite you to havin' something on the house."

Rosen turned around and saw a Chinese with sunglasses on standing beside the cash register, bowing and gesturing lavishly toward the expanse of the bar. Rosen smiled, nodded with aristocratic graciousness as he had seen people do in movies, turned back to the bartender and ordered another Scotch, and quickly finished the one in his hand. How fine people really were! How they loved their artists! Shit, man, this is the greatest country in the world.

He stirred the gift Scotch, whose ice cubes seemed just a little clearer than the ones he had paid for. How come his refrigerator never made such clear ice cubes? Vaguely he heard people entering the restaurant behind him. With no warning, he was suddenly aware that three or four couples were at the bar alongside him and that in the restaurant part, the white linen tablecloths were now alive with moving hands, plates, cigars. He held his watch up to his eyes. The undrunk part of his brain read the time. He'd finish this drink and stroll over to Palatine's. If he only had a pin for his shirt cuff.

"Excuse me."

He turned on the stool and faced a small man with very fair skin, wearing a gray-checked coat and highly polished black shoes. He was a short, round man, and Rosen realized that he himself was the same size and even the same age, just about, and he was not sure suddenly that he could ever again write a script.

The short man had a manner, it was clear, the stance of a certain amount of money. There was money in his pause, and the fit of his coat and a certain ineffable condescension in his blue eyes, and Rosen imagined a woman, no doubt the man's wife, also short, wrapped in mink, waiting a few feet away in the crowd at the bar, with the same smug look.

After the pause, during which Rosen said nothing, the short man asked, "Are you, Bernie Rosen?"

"That's right," Rosen said, and the alcohol made him sigh for air.

"You don't remember me?" the short man said, a tiny curl of a smile on the left edge of his pink mouth.

Rosen sobered. Nothing in the round face stuck to any part of his memory, and yet he knew he was not all this drunk. "I'm afraid not. Who are you?"

"You don't remember me?" The short man asked with genuine surprise.

"Well, who are you?"

The man glanced off, not so much embarrassed as unused to explaining his identity, but swallowing his pride, he looked back at Rosen and said, "You don't remember Maxie Goldstein?"

Whatever suspicion Rosen felt was swept away. Clearly, he had known this man somewhere, sometime. He felt the debt of the forgetter. "Maxie Goldstein. I'm awfully sorry, but I can't recall where. Where did I know you?"

"I sat next to you in English four years? At Roosevelt High School!"

Rosen's brain had long ago drawn a blind down on all his high-school years. But the name Goldstein did rustle the fallen leaves at the back of his mind. "I remember your name, ya, I think I do."

"Oh, come on, guy, you don't remember Maxie Goldstein with the curly red hair?" He tilted his head forward to reveal a shiny bald spot and the vestiges of remaining red hair. But no irony showed in his eyes, which were transported back to his famous blazing hair and to the seat he had had next to Bernie Rosen in high school. He smiled a very satisfying smile.

"Forgive me," Rosen said, "I have a terrible memory. I remember your name, though."

Goldstein, obviously put out, perhaps even angered but still trying to smile, and certainly full of intense sentimental interest, said, "We were best friends."

Rosen laid a beseeching hand on Goldstein's gray coat sleeve. "I'm not doubting you; I just can't place you for the moment. I mean, I believe you." He laughed.

Goldstein seemed assuaged now, nodded, and said, "You don't look much different, you know? I mean, except for the beard, I'd know you in a minute."

"Yeah, well..." Rosen said, but still feeling he had offended, he obediently asked, "What do you do?" Preparing for a long tale of success.

Goldstein clearly enjoyed this question, and he lifted his eyebrows to a proud peak. "I'm in men's clothing," he said.

A laugh began to bubble up in Rosen's stomach; Goldstein's coat was, in fact, ill-fitting. He may be successful in business, but that didn't extend to himself and his own clothing. And the importance which Goldstein attached to his profession killed the faintest smile on Rosen's face. "Really," he said with appropriate solemnity.

"Oh, yes. I'm the general sales manager for the third biggest men's clothing line in terms of sales, head of everything West of the Mississippi."

"Don't say. Well, that's wonderful." Rosen felt great relief. It would have been awful if Goldstein had been a failure—or in charge of Santa Monica only. "I'm glad you've done so well."

Goldstein glanced off to one side, letting his achievement sink deeply into Rosen's mind. When he looked again at Rosen, he could not quite keep his eyes from the frayed cuffs of the corduroy jacket and the limp shirt cuff hanging out. "What do you do?" he asked.

Rosen looked into his drink. Nothing occurred to him. He touched his finger against the mahogany bar, and still, nothing came to him through his shock. His resentment was clamoring in his head; he recognized it and greeted it. Then he looked directly at Goldstein, who in the pause had grown a look of benevolent pity. "I'm a writer," Rosen said and watched for the publicity-distorted freeze to grip Goldstein's eyeballs.

"That so!" Goldstein said, amused. "What kind of writing you do?"

If I had any style, Rosen thought, I would shrug and say I write part-time poems after I get home from the post office and would leave Goldstein to enjoy his dinner. On the other hand, I do not work in the post office, and there must be some way to shake this monkey off and get back to where I can talk to people again as if I were honest. "I write movies," he said to Goldstein.

"That so!" Goldstein smiled, his amusement enlarging toward open condescension. "Anything I would have seen or heard of?"

"Well, as a matter of fact, you might have seen...." He paused. Then he mentioned his first script, which few people saw.

"Really? That was a movie? I didn't see it, I'm afraid." Goldstein's face split into its parts; his mouth still kept its smile, but his eyes showed a certain disbelief.

"Then I wrote another one," Rosen said and paused again, tasting a bitterness on his tongue.

Goldstein's mouth opened. His skin reddened. Slowly he said, "Nope, I didn't see that either."

"And I had two out last year." Rosen named them.

The two smash hits seemed to open before Goldstein's face like bursting flats. His finger lifted toward Rosen's chest. "Are you...

Bernie Rosen?" he whispered.

"Yes."

Goldstein held out his hand tentatively. "Well, I'm delighted to meet you," he said with utter formality and reverence.

Rosen saw distance locking into place between them, and in an instant, wished he could take Goldstein in his arms and wipe out the poor man's metaphysical awe, smother his defeat, and somehow retract this very hateful pleasure, which he knew now he could not part with anymore. He shook Goldstein's hand and then covered it with his left hand.

"Really," Goldstein went on, "I truly admire you and think…. " Withdrawing his hand as though it would be caught in a trap, he said, "I… I've enjoyed your—excuse me."

Rosen's heavy cheeks glowed rose red as the sound of flatulence cut the conversation off and his mouth stirred vaguely toward a smile.

Goldstein closed his coat and quickly turned about and hurried to the little crowd waiting for tables near the red entrance door. He took the arm of a short woman in a long skirt and turned her toward the door. She seemed surprised as he hurried her out of sight and into the street

ABOUT THE AUTHOR

John Corral

John Corral is an award-winning author of mysteries, thrillers, suspense, legal dramas, and westerns. He also co-wrote and edited women's stories of love and life with Tanya Angel, and contributed and edited poetry with Ian Lewis and Iris Mede.

Books by the author include SERIAL SINS OF SIBERIA, LUST, LIES, AND LOVE, GETTING SADDAM'S GOLD, LOVE TIMES ELEVEN, THE GRISLY EFFECTS OF GREEN, DID HOLLYWOOD CAUSE THE CUBAN MISSILE CRISIS?, HIS FINAL RESTING PLACE: ELVIS, REDHEADS ARE RELENTLESS, DELPHINA: VOODOO QUEEN, 30 FLASHES OF FICTION, 15 FLASHES OF FICTION, 15 MORE FLASHES OF FICTION, MYSTERY AND MALICE, IMPERFECT KILLING, PROSECUTION MISCONDUCT, REMEMBERING DIXIE, BEYOND THERE BE DRAGONS and THE MOST DANGEROUS MAN IN THE WORLD

Books with Tanya Angel include THE SECRET LIVES OF SMILES, THE DUCHESS, WHERE THE HEART IS, and WHEN THE HEART LAUGHS IT SHOW AND WHEN IT DOESN'T IT SHOWS EVEN MORE.

Books with Ian Lewis and Iris Mede include FLOWING LIQUID LIFE, DREAMS OF A PERPETUAL DREAMER, EVOLVING LOVE, LET

LOVE FLOAT, ORDINARY LIVES EXTRAORDINARY LOVES, LET LOVE LEAD THE WAY, REAL PASSIONS REAL LOVE, LOVE THAT CHANGES EVERYTHING, THE SENSE OF SORROWS PAST, LOVE DEVILISH LOVE DIVINE, TALKING DIRTY ABOUT DESIRE, LOVE WORTH REMEMBERING, THE PLEASURES AND PAIN OF LOVE, WHEN LOVE LIFTS YOU HIGH, and WHEN LOVE SIZZLES.

John is also the author of TWO BROTHERS, a western, 3 LIFE LESSONS, an essay, and SEEING YOU, a book of poetry.

BOOKS BY THIS AUTHOR

Prosecution Misconduct

These are stories about lawyers. Some of the lawyers are highly ethical and hardworking, the kind that you'd want to have represent you if you ever got into a scape. Others are not so good -- either morally or in terms of competence. In fact, a few are the kind that give all lawyers a bad reputation. Having practiced law for over twenty-five years, I've known both types and the vast majority were of the first kind. But, alas, the ones that most often come to mind are the latter. Well, at least they were memorable enough to give me material for these stories. The downside is that they are lawyers who may sue. I say, go for it! Truth is my defense.

Potpourri: A Mixture Of Short Stories, Flash Fiction And Poetry

This is a collection of short stories, flash fiction and poetry, that, like potpourri, is a mixture of different things, scented and spiced. They are here, as in a bowl, placed to provide the reader with small samples of the ordinary anxieties and passions of life. In this collection, you will meet kings and paupers, dreamers and devils, the young and the not so young. They appear in a great variety of interesting pieces, that, in the end, are life-affirming and heart-warming, most with some funny twists.

The Colors Of Love, Life And Death: And Other Short Fiction

This book of short stories provides a range of topics and characters that have the thread of these three aspects: Love, Life, and Death. Some present love as its main topic, in its many forms; still other detail the harsh realities of life that include death. The eight short stories offer a detailed glimpse of these and transport the reader to other places and other lives presenting life lessons as well.

Two Pandemic Deaths: And Other Stories Of Love And Loss

The story that begins this collection of short fiction pieces is not true. Well, it is not entirely untrue. It was written after the loss of a dear friend, to whom it is dedicated. The sentiments expressed there are also, to some degree, present in the other stories offered here. They were written in somewhat the same melancholy mood. But let that not deter you. For great loss, there must have been great love first, that expands and fills the heart and then breaks the very thing it filled, leaving a hole that may never be fixed.

Black Oaks: A Ghost Story Novel

Do you believe in ghosts? Doesn't everyone? I certainly do based on my own experience. This novel was inspired by real events, accounts of ghosts recorded by others, and that happened to me. It is part fact and fiction; the thin line of truth between the two unidentifiable. Is this proof of an afterlife? Perhaps. There is a reason why ghost stories in classic literature are so plentiful. They are meant to comfort, as well as to instill fear. For many, encounters with the unknown are not fiction. Sometimes these encounters take the form of a reunion with a deceased loved one or a confrontation with a strange creature. Scariest of all, our inner demons may haunt us in our most troubled times. No matter how they manifest, paranormal encounters are very real for those who experience them.

Serial Sins Of Siberia: And Other Stories

The title selection in this book of short stories, Serial Sins of Siberia, concerns Russia; as does a second, Cold War Comrades: Greene and Philby. But the other five stories do not. And they differ in length, subject matter, genre, and theme. The only thing that binds them together is that they are not boring. Each is memorable and unique in its own way. And though it may seem as if they are non-fiction, given the first-person point of the narrative for some, they are not.

They take the reader from the streets of Los Angeles to the work camps of Siberia, from the notes of a CIA operative to the musing of a retiring attorney. They describe a joyful, complex, ever-changing relationships between a renown writer and a British spy, a lawyer and a porn star; the inner thoughts an avid skier, as well as the whimsical wording of a sale ad for law books; a woman confides in the reader a family secret, and you'll learn of a place where you can be either married and divorced, though not both on your same visit. Each piece showcases different views of life, and differences in individuals. Enjoy!

Lust, Lies And Love: Twenty Tales Of Love Gone Bad

These are stories about love. Not love that is sweet and tender, sublime and true, and has as little in common with reality as unicorns playing in a garden. Things don't always go as people want them to, and, in particular, when it comes to love. A lot of bad things happen instead, things that people may be ashamed of, or worse.

But there is also love in these stories. Some of them, anyway.

There is the love of long-term couples, there is the love of newly discovered lovers, and there is the love of friends. There is affection —between lovers, between colleagues, between strangers encountered on the street. There is respect: for love, for desire, for scars, for the complicated places where love and desire overlap. Above all, there is respect for love itself. That to strive for love, and have it —even for a moment, is reason enough to continue to seek it.

Getting Saddam's Gold: And Other Short Fiction

The short stories in this collection were written over the last decade. One appeared in an obscure anthology, another was published in an online magazine, and the remainder are new and original to this anthology. All of them are primarily adventure stories. That is, character and theme are incidental to the plot. Things happen, as opposed to a piece that is a character study or where some idea or interpretation of events is paramount. The object was to tell a good story —unusual and interesting, hopefully, and not moralize about its significance.

The Grisly Effects Of Green: And Nineteen Other Flash Fiction Stories

For those who already love flash fiction —exceptionally short stories— this book offers you another opportunity to indulge in your passion. For those just now discovering flash fiction, this book introduces you to a true phenomenon in recent fiction trends.

Stories have been growing shorter and shorter, for decades breaking down the conventions of longer fiction. Why? Because flash fiction captures what longer forms can't.

So what exactly does flash fiction do, or capture? As one writer noted, flash fiction can bring you awareness of a point faster and more deeply felt, then, foregoing any novelistic wind-down, leave you there suspended in that wonderful moment of recognition.

It's been said that flash fiction can do in a page what a novel does in two hundred; and, perhaps more humbly, that flash fiction is as intense as poetry, because readers who like to skip can't skip in a one-page story.

This collection provides the full span of this new phenomenon. The length of the entries ranges from one paragraph to nine pages, and includes several poems. They also vary in genre, from humor to mystery, romance to the macabre. And they can go deep; effectively changing you almost before you know it.

Did Hollywood Cause The Cuban Missle Crisis? And Other Alternative History Stories

These stories are historical fiction. Some are satire and others profoundly serious. Yet they are all plausibly written with facts and events used as the basis for more speculative narratives and alternative accounts of how history might have played out. They provide probable explanations for events or situations that might otherwise be perplexing. Some may call these conspiracy theories, implying falsification or sinister motives. They are neither. Rather, they are reinterpretations of history.

Redheads Are Relentless: And Other Stories

This book is filled with stories, each small windows into the lives of others, their minds, their hearts, and their dreams. The stories are journeys away from your own life to theirs, and back again. Some stories are fantastical and some entirely ordinary; most though are somewhere in-between. Not a single one is the same as another. We are all unique in some way and each person in this world is living a different existence; each life composed of countless stories. Nevertheless, the stories here share one thing: there are truths to be found there. Make that journey and you will bring back something you never expected.

His Final Resting Place: Elvis

This book is both a memoir and a portrait of a man who has been written about by many people. Yet this book is unique in many ways. If the person who tells the story is to be believed, Elvis Presley lived on in spirit after his body was laid to rest.

Who is this person who claims that? Who is Marilou Lipsey, the pseudonym she gave herself? Was she really jessi, the name she said Elvis sometimes used to call her?

'Marilou Lipsey' was a neighbor of mine when I lived in North Hollywood, California in the early Eighties. I learned she had "dated" Elvis, but she never said much more about that. We were casual friends only, and I moved away after a few months. About twenty-five years ago she contacted me after she learned I had written a book and said she had a story to tell me that I could publish, but only after her death. That unfortunate event just occurred and thus I am publishing it now. The following is based on what she told me over the course of several days which she said were true events. You be the judge as to the veracity of her story.

—-John Corral

Love Times Eleven: A Bittersweet Collection Of Stories

This is a collection of stories about love, in many aspects, in many lengths, and in many forms. The only unifying thread to these stories is the intense emotion of love. But, as you will learn, that may occur in a variety of ways as shown by these eleven separate stories involving a wide variety of individuals, many of whom are shown to be interlinked as the tales progress.

15 More Flashes Of Fiction: A Collection Of Short Stories

This is a collection of 15 more fiction pieces, short to very short in length, but long on the truths of life, its dramas and dangers, and its randomness. The only real thread that runs through them is their tightness and precision. Yet Plot and character development are not sacrificed in favor of compression and theme. From the author of 30 Flashes of Fiction comes another highly readable collection.

15 Flashes Of Fiction: A Collection Of Short Stories

This is a diverse mix of fiction pieces, short to very short in length, but long on the truths of life, its dramas and dangers, and its randomness. The only real thread that runs through them is their tightness and precision. Yet Plot and character development are not sacrificed in favor of compression and theme. From the author of 30 Flashes of Fiction comes another highly readable collection.

30 Flashes Of Fiction: The Idea Came Like A Flash Of Lightning And In An Instant A Truth Was Revealed --Nicola Tesla

Flash fiction is a challenge to an author and requires an immediate connection with the reader to tell a compelling story in a very short form. Ernest Hemingway is credited with its origination when he presented this as the quintessential flash fiction example:

"For sale: baby shoes, never worn."

The following 32 stories strive for that kind of effect, though they are not able to match the succinctness of Hemingway. The key is often what is left out, and which the reader supplies. No genre is neglected in this collection, and the stories range from mystery to romance, and thriller to humor. Brevity is the key, in both story and character, with the point of the story realized very quickly. Let the stories move you, inspire you and entertain you. They are intended to tell important stories, in the most abbreviated form possible. Read, and see if they convince you of that.

Beyond There Be Dragons

When the ancient mapmakers got to the edge of the known world, they used to write, "Hic Sunt Dracones," the Latin equivalent of "Beyond there be dragons." And those old maps -- early modern European maps-- illustrated the warning for the uncharted territory with beasts rumbling and where serpents writhe. Dragons lurked beyond the familiar and safe, magical creatures that were not to be taken lightly. The same warning can be applied to this collection of short stories. While they don't include one dragon per se, they certainly deal with the unknown beyond our safe, everyday lives. Thus, be forewarned: Beyond there be dragons!

The Most Dangerous Man In The World

About the collection:

In the story My Sweet Nightmare a man obtains the power to exact revenge on those who anger and vex him, but at what price?

Not of This Earth is a story of a woman who was placed here as a child to ward off the invading Dreagans. She is a Protectant, but older now and few of her kind remain.

In Vince the Second an uncommonly good poker player has always been able to "read" his opponents. Does this skill also allow him to sense approaching danger?

The Chosen One is an homage to The Lottery. Yes, there are places where this ritual is still practiced.

The Most Dangerous Man in the World recounts the arrival at a super-max prison of a homicidal killer. One reporter knows full well why he is "the most dangerous man in the world."

The Tale of Winston and Sarah is a story that confirms the old adage that "hell hath no fury like a woman scorned."

In A Dream a recurring dream of a small girl becomes too real to be just an ordinary dream.

Deathly Serious Slapstick is a story that takes place on Mars and involves The Three Stooges...seriously.

Remembering Dixie And Other Stores

About the collection: These are stories that focus on a rite of passage. They are personal stories that may seem autobiographical, but they are not. Each one, though, contains a fragment of memory that serves as a theme around which the story was built. If there is a common thread it is that someone is transformed, through love and loss, fear and distrust, hope or despair -- the mix of emotions that accompany all such transformations.

Seeing You

Seeing You is a collection of poems and flash fiction on a myriad of subjects. This book is meant to take every individual reader on their own personal emotional journey. Delve into them with their unique views on the stages of our lives; Childhood, Friendship, Love, Love Lost, Death and Rebirth. Each piece is different with thought provoking statements and questions.